Freed by The Pack

OMEGA FOR THE PACK
BOOK EIGHT

LAYLA SPARKS

Content Guide

If you don't have any triggers, please skip this page to avoid spoilers! For any questions regarding triggers, please email: author_laylasparks@yahoo.com.

~ Non-con (not glorified or by her pack- Chapter 15)
   ~ Mention of suicide (Chapter 28)
   ~ Edging
   ~ Pregnancy
   ~ Group Play
   ~ Backdoor play
   ~ Claiming bites

One

OLIVIA

Opening my eyes to the bright sunlight, I looked at the two alphas sleeping on either side of me with dread. Their muscular thighs pressed against my naked ones while the blond alpha's hand lay on my belly.

Slowly removing his hand, I sat up. I didn't want to wake them. I needed time to myself. The alphas assigned to me at the breeding camp weren't necessarily cruel - I just didn't want to go into heat and have babies for them. To just be an incubator for these alphas.

Gosh, I needed a break from this breeding camp. Every day, I prayed I wouldn't go into heat, but I knew I wouldn't be safe forever. Once they matched me to an alpha pack that I couldn't resist, my heat would come in full force.

I knew it for a fact.

Suddenly, I heard shouts and the sound of glass shattering from across the hall. *Oh my god, was that Lacy?* I shot up from the bed, and the two alphas stirred awake.

"Where are you going?" one of them asked. He was up and alert, standing behind me as I pulled my door open.

My heart beat faster when I saw Lacy's room and a crew of

males crowding the entrance. She was screaming. My heart pounding, I rushed across the hallway before my alpha handler could grab me. When I peeked in, I could see a window smashed open and alphas shifting into werewolf forms, jumping out the window. I could do nothing but watch as the guards shifted and jumped out after her.

She had fucking escaped with her pack. *Without me.* Lacy was my only hope, and I thought she would have planned this with me. I would have woken up earlier and ditched the alpha handlers if she told me to.

"Let's go," the alpha told me, trying to grab my arm. But when I heard the gunshots outside, we all froze.

My heart sank with intense dread, and I wanted to throw up.

Was my cousin still alive? My alpha handler rushed out of the room, and I was left alone in Lacy's room as I stared out the window, trying to catch a glimpse of her. Heart pounding in my chest, I ran downstairs in my pajamas and to the front lobby. I had to find her.

Alphas in full uniform stood at the entrance with guns strapped to their shoulders.

"Go to your room," said Henry, eyes flashing as he paced the lobby. Then to his henchmen. "Make an intercom announcement for all omegas to stay in their rooms today. We have a situation."

An alpha guard grabbed me by the arm before I could argue or run out of the building.

"Please, my cousin is out there!" I screamed. "She could be dead right now. You don't want omegas dead, right?"

"If only you knew," he said, his lips turning up in a sneer, and then I knew that he couldn't care less. He shoved me into my room and closed the door without a word. I screamed and ran to the door, trying to twist the doorknob open.

He had locked it from the outside.

"Let me out!" I yelled, jiggling the doorknob.

I felt the familiar sense of depression weighing over me. I suddenly felt alone. I rushed to my window and saw how high it was from the ground. I couldn't see anything except the ocean crashing against the shore of Howl's Edge. Lacy couldn't be dead. She had to be alive. And for my sanity, I refused to believe she was hurt.

I'm sure she had escaped with her bodyguard alphas. They were a strong group, and they were overprotective of her.

I paced around the room, jittery and nervous. Then, an intercom announcement came over the loudspeaker:

"All omegas, please remain in your rooms. We will let you know when it is safe to leave. We have a situation. Once again, please remain in your rooms."

Hands shaking, I decided to make my bed while I waited until they released us from our rooms. I couldn't help the tears that flowed down my face as I made the bed. My family was probably worried sick about me now, but I hoped Lacy would tell them I was fine here even though I truly wasn't.

I lifted my pillow, and a small gray pill caught my eye. Somebody had set it perfectly underneath the pillow.

What the hell?

Remembering there was a camera in the room, I quickly snatched the pill while there was a disturbance going on outside, and I rushed into the bathroom. Opening my fingers, I stared at the pill in the palm of my hand.

It was a heat suppressant pill.

I quickly downed it, grateful to have some protection against my heat arriving. But the real question was...*who left it there?* I wondered if it was a total accident or if an alpha was watching out for me.

LATER THAT MORNING, after we were finally allowed out of our rooms, I kept an eye out for the alphas who had spent time in my room last night. I couldn't see them anywhere, so I went into the Social Room feeling anxious about my cousin Lacy and her escape.

"You look pretty shaken," said Julie, pouring scrambled eggs into her plate next to me. I desperately wanted to talk to someone about it, but I wasn't sure whether I could trust her or not.

"My cousin escaped," I said, unable to keep it to myself, and her eyes widened. "There were gunshots outside and everything. I don't even know if she's alive."

"Oh my god, I hope she doesn't get caught," said Julie, flipping back her long blond hair. She loved it here at the Omega Breeding Camp or the OBC. She was living here with her younger sister, Treasure, and they believed it to be the greatest place on earth. I had no idea how they lived before this, so I wasn't one to judge. I hadn't even been here a week, and I couldn't stand it.

"I hope so, too," I sighed. "If anything happened to her, I would never forgive myself."

"I'm sure she's okay. No wonder our rooms were locked this morning," said Julie thoughtfully as we made our way to a large floor cushion.

I only had a bagel on my plate with some cream cheese. I didn't have an appetite at all, but I didn't want to raise attention to myself by not eating. Henry had a keen eye for omegas who weren't feeling well or were in heat.

"Yeah, it feels like a damn prison in here," I said, and Julie raised her eyebrows, not saying anything to my outburst. If she said something, I wouldn't know how to contain my honest views on this place. I wondered if any other omega in this place felt like I did. *Or were they all brainwashed?*

I scanned the room, looking for the alphas from last night.

Once in a while, groups of alphas would stroll inside the Social Room to mingle with the omegas, which was encouraged to bring omegas to heat. The problem was that I ignored the faces of the alphas who cuddled me the night before. "I hope Lacy does something to save us if she escapes."

"That wouldn't be so great," said Julie, heartily eating as she watched her younger sister talking with omegas who looked to be in her age group. "I would have to make sure my sister finds a good pack before I could ever get mated."

"Why is that?" I asked, astonished. I didn't have brothers or sisters, so this was new to me.

"If I get mated off to a pack, who would protect her?" said Julie. "Certainly not our parents. I'm responsible for her."

"Oh, damn," I said. "I'm sorry to hear that."

I was curious to know why her dads wouldn't protect them, but I was nervous about prying too much. I didn't want to lose my only friend in this horrible place. My worst fear was being lonely here and completely forgotten by everyone. And the only hope I had was Lacy getting help for me if she eventually managed to get home.

Suddenly, the back of my neck prickled, and I felt like someone was watching me. I turned slightly to see an alpha with short, wavy black hair gazing at me from across the room as he talked to another alpha with blond hair.

I blinked. I remembered him from last night and this morning, and he looked familiar.

He held my gaze for a few seconds before walking out of the room. *Was it he who left the pill for me?* I didn't dare get up and approach him to ask. Because if I said anything and I was wrong about him, I could get the alpha in serious trouble. And I didn't want the pills to stop coming, either.

"What's wrong?" asked Julie.

"Nothing," I said, quickly looking away from him. She couldn't know anything about the pills because of her loyalty to the OBC. And there was no way I was ruining my chances of escape.

∼

THAT NIGHT, I lay in bed eagerly waiting to see who my alpha handlers would be for tonight.

It was the first time I was actually looking forward to it, so I already had stripped down to nothing with the white bedsheet pulled over my body and tucked underneath my chin. This time, it seemed to be taking forever, and I looked at the clock, hoping for it to become nine p.m. already.

After a few minutes, I heard the two men step into my room, and my eyes shot open. The same alpha from last night with the curly black hair and intense gaze was back. And his blond friend with long locks of hair. One of them was responsible for leaving the heat suppressant under my pillow, and tomorrow morning, I'd know for sure.

"Hi," I said shakily. I still wasn't used to this shit. I never cuddled with naked grown alphas before being kidnapped and brought to this camp. After they stripped off their black bathrobes, they silently slid under the bedsheet on both sides of me.

"Hello, Olivia," said the black-haired one. His voice was like a breeze in my ear, gentle and rolling. *Was I noticing all this because he might've left me the heat suppressant pill?*

But I couldn't ask him that, especially with the cameras on the ceiling above us.

They got comfortable pressing their bodies against mine, creating a nest of warmth against me. My breathing grew harsher, and my breasts pressed against the black-haired alpha while the blond one spooned me from behind.

"What's your name?" I asked breathlessly. I swear if I

didn't see the pill tomorrow morning, I would never waste another second of my time with this alpha.

"Sergio," he answered, staring at me with hooded eyes. His jawline stood out in the moonlight with his ultra-serious expression, and he looked like he couldn't be bothered to talk.

The alpha behind me didn't seem to like being ignored.

"My name's Ian, if you're wondering," he said, and my face cracked into the first smile in days.

"Nice to meet you, Ian," I said, even though my mind was racing about the pill they left this morning. Because I could have sworn it wasn't there before.

"You seem to be on edge," observed Sergio. "You need to relax in order to go into heat."

What?! But wasn't he the one who left me the heat suppressant?

It definitely wasn't him then.

"Yeah, sure," I said, shutting down again. I closed my eyes and turned onto my back so none of them could see my face directly. Their mission was to get me into heat and nothing else. I should never have thought I'd have a chance to escape with an alpha's help.

"What's wrong?" asked Ian.

"I don't want to go into heat," I said vehemently as they rubbed my arms and thighs. Their breaths on my neck were causing my pulse to skyrocket, and the clenching of my pussy sent alarm bells through me. If I went into heat in this place, there would be absolutely no hope left.

"Why not?" asked Sergio suddenly, and his hand tightened on my wrist. I looked over at him and noticed his eyes on the camera. Chills went through me. He was acting like an asshole for the security camera. "An omega should *want* to go into heat and have babies with her future mates."

"Because I have dreams," I said.

"What kind of dreams?"

I didn't feel like getting too personal, but if I wanted those heat suppressant pills, I'd better fight for my case.

"I always wanted to be a writer, you know?" I whispered. I didn't tell many people this information for fear of being ridiculed. I was twenty-four, and yet I still haven't been able to hold down a real job, except for being a part-time receptionist at the Howl's Honor Hospital and writing on the side. I had notebooks full of half-finished stories, and my dream was to finish writing an entire book.

"That's amazing," he said, his eyes still on the camera. "But you can still have babies at the same time."

Two

OLIVIA

The next morning, my heart pounded in my chest as I brushed my teeth.

I was eager to check under my pillow after the alphas left. They usually left around this time, and I would finally get my answer.

Drying my face with the hand towel, I quickly left the bathroom and pulled on a bathrobe to cover my naked body. Once I was sure the door was locked and they'd left, I casually walked to the bed just in case someone was watching me through the cameras.

I picked up my pillow, and sure enough, the pill with the gray matter floating inside sat there. My heart leaped in my throat as I slowly curled my fingers around it underneath the pillow. My heart pounded as I walked back into my bathroom in the rooms they assigned for us omegas.

Downing the pill with a handful of water, I was safe, at least for another day. These pills would prevent me from going into heat because if I went into heat, I would be a pain-ridden omega, intent on getting fucked by multiple alphas until I was impregnated. I'd never been knotted before or even had sex, so the thought terrified me. I had kissed deltas and betas in the past, but never with alpha in case they went into a rut and knotted me.

I combed my shoulder-length curly and unruly black hair as I stared in the mirror, lost in thought. I would have to pretend everything was normal because I didn't want to raise any suspicion and ruin all my chances of escaping. I contemplated running straight out the front door, but these were alphas. They were lean, fast, and vicious, especially when they hunted for an omega. They would hunt for me until the end of time, and the thought sent chills radiating through my body. I was curious why Sergio or Ian left me the heat suppressant pill. *Wouldn't they want me to go into heat so they could rut me to their heart's desire?*

It didn't make sense to me, and I was determined to find out.

During lunchtime, I was surprised to see a bunch of alphas coming into the Social Room to mingle with the omegas. They sat on the cushions, holding omegas on their laps and breathing down their necks.

I shuddered, watching them.

"There's a lot of them today," I whispered to Julie.

"They all come in here twice a week," she said, her eyes settling on a certain alpha with glasses. He was also staring at her from across the room, and her cheeks turned pink with delight.

"You like him," I said, thinking it was cute but not so cute considering the situation we were in.

We were pretty much kidnapped to be bred by these alphas.

"I *do* like him," she said, her face turning redder.

I didn't see Sergio anywhere in the room, and I wondered where he might be. He was an interesting alpha and the gentlest one by default. But an alpha with short blue hair was standing in the corner of the room, his eyes darting between the omegas, landing on me occasionally.

"Who's that?" I asked. When his eyes landed on me again, an eerie feeling settled over me, causing me to look away immediately.

"Oh, that's Brett," she said. "The omegas know to steer clear of him. He's not the easiest alpha handler to be with."

"What do you mean?"

"Well, there's a rumor- don't quote me on it. But there's a rumor that he's the one they use to discipline rowdy omegas," she said, and that made my heart pound faster with fear.

"They discipline omegas?"

"Yes, but only the ones who try to escape or do anything sneaky that's against the rules," said Julie. "I'm going to say hi to Matthew."

"Have fun," I said, shaking my head as I watched her shamelessly walk up to him to flirt.

Suddenly, I caught sight of Sergio walking in through the door, and his eyes immediately locked onto mine. It was like a thunderbolt shooting right through me when we made eye contact. It was magnetic when I stood up from the cushions and made my way over to him without thinking. I had to ask him if he was the one who left me the pills. I had to know if I had any chance of escaping out of this hellhole. He looked surprised when I stood before him, my arms crossed.

"Hello, Olivia," he greeted. His gentle voice was a different baritone than any other alpha I met, and I didn't get sick of listening to it.

"Hey, Serg," I said. "I mean Sergio."

"You can call me whatever you want, honey."

"Okay," I said, now frazzled at being called 'honey.' His eyes were intelligent, and he looked at me like I was on equal footing with him and not some piece of meat. "I have a question for you."

"Yes?"

"Was it you?"

"I don't quite understand what you mean?" he said, looking at me with amusement in his eyes. But the nervous swallow in his throat gave him away.

And I instantly knew.

"Why did you do it? Is there any chance of me getting out of here?"

"I have no idea what you're talking about," he said with finality, his jaw hardening as he looked away from me. That pissed me off. We were in a crowd full of people, and there was no reason why he couldn't disclose that he was the one giving me the heat suppressants. The room was loud enough, and no one would hear him.

"Oh, okay, whatever," I said, rolling my eyes.

I huffed as I stomped away from him.

I suddenly felt alone and not sure what to do with myself. I needed some air since this enormous room that looked like a cafeteria was flooded with alpha and omega scents that played havoc on my hormones. When I was finally out of there, I walked down the hall and towards the spa area. There were doors marked as a massage room, and I decided that a good massage might help me.

I have been on edge ever since I was here, and the only moment I relaxed was when my cousin Lacy was here. But now she escaped, and I was completely and utterly alone in this damn place in the middle of nowhere. The massage room was small when I walked in, and there wasn't anyone in there. The room was empty except for a bed with towels, a chair next to it, and instructions on the wall. I read through it, and I was supposed to press the green button on the bed when I was fully stripped down.

Removing my dress but leaving my underwear and bra on, I lay on the bed and pressed the green buzzer-looking thing on the head of the bed.

I flopped my head to the side, waiting. It would feel amazing to have a full body massage and get lost in another world for at least thirty minutes until I decided what to do because there was no way I was going to stay here forever.

The door opened with a squeak, and I suddenly felt large, warm hands on my shoulders.

"Whoa," I said out loud, turning and sitting up in alarm. It was Sergio standing there, staring at me nonchalantly.

"It's okay, don't be scared," he said in a calm baritone with his hand on my back. "I'm here to give you a massage. It's encouraged for alphas to massage the omegas, and I happened to get the call."

"Oh, umm," I said, shifting awkwardly back onto my stomach. "I guess, but nothing freaky, okay?"

"Of course," he chuckled softly, and my face warmed. I would use this chance to question him further and figure it out without getting myself in trouble that I took the heat suppressant pills. "I'm going to put a little oil on you. Don't be alarmed."

"Okay," I said, laying my head back down, trying to relax but also very aware that my butt was hanging out and barely covered in the tiny underwear they provided. If they were a couple of sizes larger, I'd be more comfortable. The scent of lavender and roses wafted in the air, calming my senses. But my natural scent of cherry filled the air with every stroke of his hand between my shoulders.

His fingers were like magic, starting with a gentle kneading motion that released the knots in my shoulders. I couldn't help but let out a contented sigh as his hands glided over my skin, tracing a path down my spine and soothing every inch of my body.

"You seem to be on edge," he whispered, lowering his head to my ear.

"Was it you?" I asked, getting straight to the point but letting out a moan when he cracked a particular area in my back that's been aching me for months. His strength was gentle and not forceful with the added pressure he applied.

"It seems that you'll never give up asking me that," he said. "But to answer your question. Yes...it was me."

"Why?"

"Because if an omega chooses not to be in heat, she should be given the option," he said slowly and quietly as his hands lowered to my spine, easing some of my tension. I was so confused now. *Wasn't it his job to impregnate omegas?*

But I wasn't complaining.

"Why do you feel that way?" I whispered, too. "Not many alphas would care if she goes into heat. They're all dumb-headed oafs."

He chuckled as he slowly massaged the back of my upper thighs next, and I knew my scent was overwhelming. His hands were turning me on like crazy, and my pussy was coming alive even without him touching it directly. Taking deep breaths, I told my mind to relax. But his alpha scent called to my inner omega wolf. Awakening her.

"I have my reasons," he said, putting an end to the conversation as soon as it started. "I have a question for you, Olivia."

"Yes?"

"How did you end up here?"

"I was kidnapped," I said. "Didn't have a fucking choice in the matter, and I'm definitely not staying here."

"You might want to be careful of who you talk to and who you tell your plans to."

"Why? Are *you* going to rat me out?"

He sighed heavily. "I'm only trying to help in what little way I can. Do not mention anything of what I gave you to anyone. If it ever comes out, we will both be at major risk. Do you understand, Olivia?"

Three

OLIVIA

"Yes, I understand," I said, my heart pounding. I didn't expect this alpha to suddenly get so serious. He continued massaging my thighs, and my heart pounded hard in my chest, wishing he'd separate them.

No, I couldn't keep thinking these thoughts.

Breathe, Olivia.

"Are you enjoying the massage?" he asked me.

"Mhm," I said, melting like chocolate underneath his fingers. Even the embarrassment of my scent being all over the place didn't bother me. I was sure he smelt many omegas during his days here. "How long have you worked as an alpha handler? If that's even a real job."

"Three years. And it's a real job."

"Do you get paid to cuddle omegas?" I asked, laughing. "That's the dream job for an alpha."

"Not if you have a conscience," he replied, and I was starting to wonder again why he was preventing me from going into heat and why he cared so much if I did.

"Have you ever had an omega to yourself? Like a pack

omega?" I asked, curious how he even got here if all he was doing was giving out heat suppressant pills to omegas without getting caught.

"I have not," he said. "Sure, I had some fun back in the day, but I had come to a new realization."

"Which is?"

"I don't want to talk about that, Liv. Do you care if I call you that for short?"

"No," I said, closing my eyes when he massaged out another kink in my lower back. "People call me Olivia, Liv, Libby."

"Alright, we're all done then, Liv," he said, rubbing his hand one last time down my back. I ached for his hand to touch my ass, just to squeeze it a little bit, but he removed his hand, and cold air replaced the warmth he created.

"Thank you," I said, slowly sitting up on the bed, trying to get my bearings. I was a little dizzy from being so relaxed in that position. I looked at the time and realized an entire half hour had passed before I even realized it. He helped me stand up, and I was a little crestfallen when his body wasn't as close to mine anymore. "Do omegas usually get different handlers each night?"

"The alpha handler will continue to bring the omega to heat if they are compatible with each other, so the process can be quicker," he explained.

"How do they know they are compatible?"

"There will be chemistry between the alpha and omega. Sparks, you can say."

"Oh," I said, not wanting to seem desperate or anything. It wouldn't even make sense to start a relationship anyways if I wanted to fucking escape. But not many males piqued my interest like him. He was well-spoken and seemed intelligent, which was such a turn-on for me. "I need to go to my room."

I quickly threw on my dress, and he led me down the hallway with a hand on the small of my back. I needed a shower badly after perfuming so much from being aroused. I could smell my cherry scent literally seeping from my pores with each step to my room. Sergio walked me all the way to my door, and I thanked him.

"I'll see you later," he said in a low voice, his gaze locked onto mine. We stood like that for thirty seconds, and I nodded, breathless, as he opened my door. "Go ahead and relax for now before you have to entertain a big dumbheaded oaf like myself."

My face cracked into a smile, and he smiled back as he left me standing there.

I burst into my room, closed the door, and held a hand to my beating heart. *What the fuck just happened?* I couldn't believe I was starting to have feelings for this mysterious alpha. But at the same time, I couldn't deny the attraction I felt for Sergio. He was nothing like any of the other alphas. Not at all. Breathing hard, I quickly stripped down, dropping the sweaty mass of cherry-scented clothes into the bin that the betas would take in the morning to wash.

I grabbed a towel and headed to the bathroom. But before I could take a step towards it, I heard a knocking at the door. The door opened, and the blue-haired alpha I'd seen in the Social Room stood there at the entrance, looking as creepy as ever.

"Oh my god!" I squealed, quickly wrapping the towel around me. I forgot what his name was.

Oh yeah. His name was Brett. The weird one.

He stepped into the room and closed the door softly with a click. His energy wasn't at all the same as Sergio's. It was more wild and aggressive. When he looked at me, he was intense, and I could see the darkness lurking just behind his gaze.

"I saw you and your friend staring at me this morning," he said in a low voice, approaching me slowly. I didn't dare move for fear he'd approach me even faster. I didn't know what to expect from this alpha. His scent was like gasoline when he stopped in front of me, lifting my chin with his finger. My pulse elevated in fear now instead of the amazing high I felt earlier with Sergio. "What were you two talking about?"

"Nothing," I said quickly, but he didn't believe me. He gripped my shoulders, leading me to the bed. "What are you doing?"

"I'm going to help you go into heat," he said with a thin smile, pushing me onto the bed and making me fall onto my back. Then he ripped my towel open and inhaled deeply, taking a whiff of my pussy. "Your scent is all over the hallways. Just calling to me."

I swallowed with dread.

~

Sergio

Damn.

Olivia was going to be a tough one to fight my feelings for. My hands missed the texture of her smooth skin as I walked away from her door and into the alpha quarters, which were on the opposite wing of the building.

She was very different than most of the omegas here.

The omegas were either very combative or extremely whiny. She was neither. She took everything in with a thoughtful acceptance that I found very attractive, even though she wasn't happy here.

When I finally reached my room, I locked the door behind me and unbuckled my silver belt, letting my pants drop down my sinewy thighs covered in black hair. I gripped my hard dick with a rag in my other hand.

My eyes closed, picturing Liv in my mind. With her on the massage table and her ass jiggling for me. I fucking craved to touch her luscious butt. To massage her thoroughly until she was completely satisfied. Gripping my cock harder, I envisioned pulling down her panties which were damp from the massage, and watching her trembling pussy respond to my every touch.

"Fuck," I said out loud when I exploded into the rag. I sat in the chair, breathing hard as I wiped my hands clean. I had to get ahold of myself around her, especially if I was going to be her handler. I couldn't let things get out of control, or else I'd unwillingly bring her to heat, which I didn't want to happen to her.

It would ruin all my purpose of being here.

After a quick shower, I pulled on my uniform, excited to finish up the rest of the day because I had Liv to look forward to. It was about two hours before it was time for the cuddle session, and I couldn't fucking wait to hold her naked body in my arms. As I buttoned up my shirt, my packmate Ian came bursting in.

"Dude," I said, shaking my head.

"I was wondering where you disappeared off to," he said, pushing back his floppy blond hair with a grin. "What were you doing?"

"It's none of your concern," I said gruffly.

"I saw your eye on that omega. The one we cuddled last night with the very curly hair."

I groaned. I didn't need him to know that I had feelings for her. It was feelings of lust and nothing more.

"Yes, so?"

"So you have feelings for her?" said Ian, grinning even more widely. "After all this time of avoiding it."

"I do not," I said. "It's dangerous to fall for an omega here."

"When is the raid happening? Aren't you supposed to be informing the Royal Pack?"

"Shut up," I growled, slamming my door shut so no one could hear. Ian knew better than to talk loudly about me working undercover for the government. There weren't cameras in the alphas' rooms, but I couldn't risk it. Ian was working undercover with me to expose this operation of breeding omegas. "It's happening soon, but I don't know exactly when. Evan is there right now."

Evan was the third alpha in my pack and took the most dangerous missions, being the actual informant. He would be back tonight with news on the latest of the outside world.

"What are you going to do once all this is over?" asked Ian. "Pick an omega for our pack?"

I sighed heavily.

"Only if she wanted to," I said, thinking instantly of Olivia and her glossy curls. I wondered what her curls looked like down there, and my cock began to instantly stir to life again. "Let's just hope it all goes well with Evan. The problem is that he doesn't have enough proof of mistreatment."

"And the only way is if one of us works at the other building," nodded Ian. "And we know for a fact that's where omegas go to die."

A heaviness settled in my soul at the thought. I had only been there on short visits, but I'd seen the mistreatment and how they were held in cells after giving birth. Then, they would be brought back to this building, devoid of excitement and energy after their baby had been taken away to foster care.

And I knew a lot about living in foster care since I was one of those children.

"Yes," I said shortly.

"Fuck, I'm sorry. I forgot," he said.

"It's fine," I said, trying to block the memories for now. My mother was the only reason I was here. "Tonight, we'll be Olivia's handlers again."

"So you're feeling something with her?"

"We're the best match for her," I said. "Without a doubt. I don't want another alpha in there with her. She deserves to be saved."

Four

OLIVIA

"Get off me!" I screamed, trying to kick him in the balls, but Brett continued to spread my legs with a wild look in his pitch-black eyes. He licked his lips and brought his mouth to my drenched pussy. He gripped my thighs tight enough to hurt to make me shut up, and I did when I couldn't take the pain anymore.

"You taste...so divine," he muttered, licking my pussy around in circles with his tongue. His tongue felt rough and wide, stimulating my clitoris, but I breathed in deeply to avoid getting horny for him.

"Please don't," I begged, but he swiped his tongue over me one more time. Then he sat up on his haunches, staring at me with eyes that looked like slits. His lips were glistening from my wetness.

"I will make a request to be your handler," he said, and my heart pounded in alarm. "I never tasted pussy this exquisite." He licked his lips and got off the bed, silently leaving my room- shutting the door behind him.

I lay there frozen.

My heart was thundering in my chest from what had just happened, and it felt like it was all a nightmare.

Did he just fucking taste me? Who was this guy? Was it even allowed?

I realized with dread that the alphas could get away with anything, and I so happened to get lucky being matched with Sergio. I turned to my side on the bed, staring into space in shock. I still couldn't believe what just happened to me. Do I even report him? But I was too scared to bring attention to myself.

I had to get in the shower and wash off everything about him.

Holding a hand to my chest, I got off the bed and went into the sterile white bathroom, making sure to lock the door. With shaking hands, I turned the shower knob until I was covered in warm water. I stood there without moving for a while, and then I slowly pushed myself to wash my body like nothing happened. But the icky feeling of his tongue between my legs didn't go away as I scrubbed myself with a soft cloth.

Wrapping my body in a towel, I leaned against the wall after my shower, trying to get my bearings. I would be fine, I thought. Worse things happened to other omegas all the fucking time, and I had to just move on. I pulled on a pair of light blue sweatpants and a black t-shirt to feel cozy, even for a little while, before I had to take it all off.

My stomach growled, but I couldn't bring myself to get dinner at seven. I didn't want to see any alphas right now, especially the blue-haired monster, Brett. I'd rather stay in my room until tomorrow morning, and maybe I'd calm down by then.

I decided to crack open a box of puzzles and play to pass the time. I knew Julie would be wondering where I was, but I'd tell her I wasn't feeling well. Sitting cross-legged on the blue rug, I poured out the puzzles, shocked at how many there were. It seemed like there were a thousand pieces, but upon inspecting the box, it was five hundred pieces.

Each piece was tiny, and a happy flutter went through me.

I loved challenges like these, and it would take my mind off what happened with Brett. As I fit each puzzle piece together, I wondered what was happening with my mother and my four alpha fathers. I knew they were missing me from what Lacy's bodyguard had told her. I missed them so much a physical ache would go through my body.

Not realizing a couple of hours had gone by, I looked up when my bedroom door opened, and I saw Sergio, Ian, and someone else, whom I hadn't met before, walk in. *Oh shit, I hadn't stripped down for the cuddle session.*

I quickly got up to do just that, but Sergio held up a hand.

"No, just relax, Liv," he said in his gentle, calming voice. "I don't want to interrupt your game here. Mind if we join you?"

"Um, sure," I said slowly, unsure if he was just joking or not. But when all three hunky alphas sat around the puzzle board, I slowly sat between them.

"You may not like this, Liv," said Sergio. "But you'll need to sit on my lap. They are always watching the cameras."

"Oh, of course," I said, awkwardly scooting towards him, but he picked me up in one swoop and set me down on his lap. "You're pretty strong if you can carry me."

He chuckled. "You're not heavy at all."

"She's sweet," said the alpha I hadn't met yet.

He was the largest of the pack, with bulging muscles, wavy black hair, and green eyes. He had one earring and a small tattoo on his face, which made him look a little intimidating, but he was hot as hell at first glance. He wasn't the typical alpha I'd go for, but if I could enjoy him for one night, I wouldn't mind at all.

"This is Evan," said Sergio, introducing me to him, and we shook hands. "Evan, this is Olivia."

"Nice to meet you," he said, his large hand caressing mine. My heart beating fast, I pulled my hand away, and he blinked at the sudden move.

"Nice to meet you too," I said quickly to cover the awkward moment. I wasn't smooth by any means, and I was almost always embarrassing myself. But I had Brett to blame for today. He had put me in a jittery mood when this was supposed to be a fun night with Sergio.

Sergio's lap was warm as they joined me in the game, piecing the puzzles together. Ian put a hand on my thigh, and my breathing accelerated instantly, which Sergio noticed.

"Liv, is everything okay?" he asked, his deep voice rumbling in my ear behind.

"Yes," I said in a shaky voice.

"I don't think so," he said. "Tell me what's wrong, little omega."

My eyes burned with unshed tears as I took in a few deep breaths. I couldn't tell him. I didn't want any drama to happen at all because of me.

I had to survive here.

"I'm just a little hungry, that's all," I said.

"We'll bring you food," said Evan. "What do you like to eat?"

"I can't ask you to do that," I protested, clutching Sergio's knee without realizing.

"He will bring food for you," said Sergio with finality.

"Anything is fine," I said.

"Okay, they made fried chicken for dinner, so I'll check in the kitchens," said Evan. "Go ahead, Ian."

"What?" said Ian, who was intensely concentrating on the puzzles and lying on his belly.

"Ian," said Evan with a low growl, and Ian sighed. I bit my lip as Ian looked at me, and he smiled.

"You're lucky you're cute as fuck," said Ian, and I looked down bashfully.

"Sorry, I don't want to be annoying. It's seriously fine. You don't have to get it," I said.

"I want to, don't worry," said Ian. "I just give my pack a hard time, that's all. I'll even cook the food for you if it comes to that."

After that declaration, he left the room, and I let out a long breath.

"Eating some food will help relax you," said Sergio, his lips near my ear. It sent the good type of shivers down my spine, nothing like the type of fear Brett aroused in me. We continued to put the puzzles together while I debated with myself whether to tell him or not. But as more time passed, I started to forget the fear I felt earlier today and instead decided to focus on the alphas with me right now.

"Your food," said Ian, coming into the room with a stacked plate.

My stomach growled immediately at the delicious aroma of chicken, and the men chuckled softly. I grabbed the plate and tried to eat each piece of chicken elegantly like a lady.

"Just relax," said Sergio.

At his words, I dropped my fork and knife, grabbed the drumstick, and took a big bite.

I didn't care anymore.

Too hungry to care, I dipped each piece of chicken into the mashed potato, eating it messily while trying to balance the plate on my lap.

Feeling something hard underneath me, I realized with shock that it was Sergio.

He was hard while I continued to eat like a fiend on his lap.

My face warmed at the thought as I continued eating, but I slowed down as I got more full. I looked up and saw that the men had already put together half the puzzle board.

"You guys are fast," I commented as I chugged down the water bottle. "I struggled for hours trying to put together five pieces."

"The puzzle pieces are too small for my fingers," complained Evan, sitting back and watching as Ian put them together like a pro. Sergio's hands cradled my waist as I ate, but once in a while, he'd see a puzzle piece and fit it in.

His cock underneath me felt like it was coming alive and growing bigger the more I ate. I started to wonder if *his* puzzle piece would fit into mine, but I couldn't think of those thoughts. Going into heat in this place would be a disaster.

Slick moisture gathered between my legs as I sat there, and I couldn't help but squirm a little on his lap to feel if it was really his penis. The small groan he released told me he was horny but trying not to show me. I jiggled my butt over him again, and more slick drenched my pussy, trailing down my inner thighs.

"You better stop that," he growled in my ear, sending butterflies to my stomach.

"I'm all done eating," I said quickly.

I hopped off his lap, my face flushed as I quickly headed to the bathroom. Washing the oil from my hands thoroughly with soap, I wondered how I would cuddle with three men instead of just two like it had always been. My face grew warmer at the thought of Evan and his handsome looks. Sergio had the brains, which attracted me immensely, but I could tell Evan might be into sports. Ian was fun to hang around with and easy to be with, which I liked. If I had to be with a pack, I enjoyed being around them.

"Sorry, I'm back," I said, blushing when they all gazed at me hungrily.

"Let's get you to bed now, Liv," said Sergio, nodding at my clothes and indicating for me to remove them. I could sense the dark passion stirring underneath his gaze as he waited for me to strip down.

Five

SERGIO

I wasn't supposed to be feeling like this, but my dick was hard as fuck while I watched the shy omega slowly remove her baggy shirt and sweatpants.

I saw the hint of her red cheeks as she blushed.

My heart thundered in my chest, watching her unhook her bra, which tumbled to the floor. Her ample pale breasts were finally freed of their constraint as she quickly pulled down her black panties.

I had to do this for the camera that was blinking high up on the ceiling. But now, it was turning into something of my own pleasure, but I couldn't allow myself to lose control around this omega who brought out the beast in me. I was shocked to see her playing puzzles, and it turned me on that she found fun in that sort of stuff. Most omegas cared more about their looks, preening themselves all day for alphas.

But this omega looked like she couldn't care less as she snuggled under the sheets and closed her eyes. Her scent of arousal wafted all around the room, and I could sense the other alphas getting antsy as they removed their robes. I stalked to the bed and dropped my robe at the foot of the bed, climbing over the sheets. Ian and Evan each took a side next to her, but I wanted to lay between her thighs. It was the position that was encouraged by Henry's protocols if there were three or more alphas in the bed with the omega. The two alphas snuggled under sheets next to her while I lay on top of the sheet so as not to alarm her. I nudged her thighs with my nose, and she bit her lip as she slowly spread her thighs so I could lay my head in the middle.

I knew the type of alphas watching through the cameras. Any infractions could get me punished or killed. Bringing an omega to heat by force didn't turn me on like it did other alphas. But we all didn't have a choice at this moment, and the only saving grace I had was the pill I would provide for her in the morning.

"Okay, this is a little cozy," she breathed while clutching the sheets to her chin. She looked adorable and snuggled between the three of us. "Do you really have to lay right there, Serg?"

I smiled while inhaling her aroused scent through the sheets.

"Yes," I said without further explanation. I couldn't risk her talking about the pill or anything to give me away while the cameras were directly above us. They watched us constantly to the point of causing paranoia with the alphas.

Evan switched off the table lamp, covering us in darkness. For a few minutes, we all quietly breathed next to her, allowing her to relax and ease any tension she felt cuddling with us. I massaged her thighs while I laid on my stomach between her legs.

Her scent was literally soaking through the sheets now, feeding the frenzy of my alpha wolf dwelling within me. I took deep breaths to try and calm down, but each intake of breathing her in made my dick harden and press against the bed. It was a good thing there was a sheet between her pussy and my mouth, or else I would have devoured her entirely.

I wondered how the fuck I was going to sleep with this raging hard-on.

"Are you comfortable?" Ian asked her as he placed his hand on her belly.

"Yes," she said in a breathy voice that made me want to instantly fuck her right then and there, ending with a big knot. Her scent was growing stronger by the minute, and she very subtly spread her thighs even more for me.

"Liv, what are you doing?" I asked, inhaling the sheet and her scent.

"I...I can't help it."

"Can't help what?"

"Do you want to taste?" she offered, hugging my head with her thighs. I took in another deep breath, recognizing the neediness of her scent and how much she needed my tongue right now.

"I can't do that," I said, conflicted. I couldn't risk bringing her to heat. She would despise me forever, and everything I did to help prevent it would be for nothing.

"Please. Sergio."

Taking in a deep breath, I couldn't resist this omega anymore. Her scent had drenched through the sheet, and she was literally begging me.

Just one little taste.

Diving under the sheet, I immediately crawled towards the middle of her thighs. In the pitch dark, I knew where her pussy was, just from her musky cherry scent. I located her sweet middle with my tongue, swirling around her wet folds.

She let out a shuddering sigh as I licked her.

Pressing my nose against her pussy, I sniffed her in deeply. Her pussy was everything and more to me at this moment. I wanted to so badly stick my cock into her and feel her tightness around me.

"You taste...amazing," I muttered against her labia. I swiped her clitoris with my tongue, and she jerked against me because of her sensitivity. Her thighs hugged my head, drawing me in closer to her. I pressed my lips against her pussy as I sucked her juices. I wanted every drop of this woman on my tongue. This extraordinary omega who captured my attention and held it.

"Fuck, I wish I was the one tasting her. Lucky bastard," muttered Evan, who was massaging her breasts. Ian was also doing the same. Her pulse rate increased and became shallower the more I tasted her exquisite pussy.

I pushed my tongue inside her, stretching her, and she cried out when I felt her barrier blocking me. She was still a virgin, and that turned me on even more. Withdrawing my tongue, I paused devouring her pussy until she whined with need.

"You're a virgin," I said. "I don't want to scare you."

"Please, you're not scaring me," she pleaded, and I immediately placed my mouth over her entire pussy, sucking her and rubbing her clit with my thumb. Her pussy squelched with every lick and swipe of my tongue.

Faster and faster, I rubbed her clit while pulling on her labia with my mouth. I sucked her dry each time she released more slick.

She began to tremble and moan. She was close to orgasm. Gripping her thighs so she didn't escape, I rubbed her clit furiously with my tongue.

"Oh, Serg!" she shouted, and I increased the pressure, simultaneously sucking every drop that seeped from her wet delicious pussy. Her cries filled the room as I slurped and swirled with my tongue on her pussy. She jerked her hips, trying to buck me off, but I held her tight to me so she didn't escape. I needed her to gush all over my face. Then she screamed, and another bout of liquid spurted straight from her pussy as she screamed.

Releasing my hold on her thighs, I licked her fluttering pussy clean, feeling the pulse of her clit on my tongue as I did so. Then I caressed her thighs as I gently licked off her remaining juices.

"Good girl," I crooned, and she let out a sigh of contentment. "You came so strongly."

"Oh," she said in wonderment. Evan chuckled with his hand still squeezing her breast.

"Was that your first time getting eaten out?" he asked.

"Yes," she said.

"I'm honored to be your first," I said. I didn't ask her why she saved herself in this way because it was pretty normal for most omegas to reserve themselves for their future alpha packs. I couldn't see her facial expression in the dark, but I could feel her mood rising with happiness and uncertainty as she laid there. "If you notice any signs of...you know. Let us know."

"Okay," she said quietly, knowing right away that I was referring to her heat. I laid on my side and kissed her inner thigh.

"Thank you for letting me taste," I said, closing my eyes. "Have a good night, Liv."

"Goodnight," she said. "I feel so relaxed."

I smiled against her thigh as I fell asleep, smelling her beautiful aroused scent permeating from her pussy all night long.

THE FOLLOWING MORNING, I removed myself from the bed to the snores of the three. I looked at Olivia one last time, admiring her content face.

I needed to be up early to take the week-long vacation that

every alpha had. I would use it to get more heat suppressant pills as I pulled the last one from the pocket of my robe. I very gently slid the pill under her pillow, trying not to wake her while covering it completely between my fingers.

From the view of the cameras, it would just look like I was caressing her face.

Leaving her room, I walked down the hallway, smiling to myself at the thought of how she opened herself up to me and allowed me to get a taste of her pussy. Tightening my robe around me, I still couldn't believe it. It wasn't something that I could easily forget, that was for sure. She was the first omega here at the breeding camp that I ever touched like that. Never did I allow myself to indulge in that sort of thing. Honestly, I didn't even want to leave this building now that I had an omega to look forward to, but it was necessary for her safety.

"Serg, how was your shift?" said Rodmon, clapping me on the shoulder as we both walked to the alphas' wing of the building. Rodmon was one of the younger alphas, still in his early twenties.

"Went pretty well," I said vaguely. *What else was there to say about cuddling a cute omega all night?* Rodmon sighed, and I turned to look at him. "What's up, man?"

"I think I'm falling for her," he said, his eyes lost as he stared down the dark hallway. "The omega I've been cuddling for the past three days."

"What's her name?"

"Treasure," he said. "Her voice is so feathery light, like smooth butter. And she's so gentle."

"It looks like you've fallen hard," I said. "You know we can't do that around here."

It wasn't rare for alphas to get attached to their omegas, but it would hurt them if the omega were to be taken away to the other building to give birth, and some were never seen again. Rodmon's face was flushed red, and he looked like he was most certainly falling for his omega.

"I can't help it," he said, rubbing the sleep from his eyes. "I don't think I'd be happy if another alpha handled her tonight."

"Ask Henry to make you her permanent handler if she's also feeling the same about you."

"Oh, she is," Rodmon sighed as I opened my room door. "Hey, I forgot you are on vacation this week. Any fun plans?"

"Not really," I said. "Probably to visit family…"

"Cool," said Rodmon. "Have a great vacation then. I'll see you when you get back."

"Thanks," I said, shutting the door and letting out a long breath. Rodmon's conversation reminded me of my own attraction to Olivia. Maybe going on vacation would be the best thing for me to forget about all the feelings that were growing between us.

I took a quick shower and pulled on a pair of casual jeans with a white shirt. I couldn't wait to tell the Royal Pack of my findings after they employed me to live here for years. I had pictures and recordings of omegas who stated they didn't want to be here. It would be a fruitful week, and hopefully, I would be able to get Olivia out of here.

I was in the middle of throwing my clothes into a small suitcase when I heard a knock on the door.

"Come in," I said, not even looking at the door. I was too preoccupied trying to fit a bunch of jeans into my suitcase without folding it.

"Well, hello, Sergio," said a silky, thin voice behind me. I groaned inside when I recognized Henry's voice. I turned and stood up to shake his hand. His eyes were dark and veiled. I never knew what to expect from the head of the omega breeding camp, but I knew one thing.

This alpha was pure evil.

Six

OLIVIA

I was too cozy to open my eyes and wake up.

The bed was warm, and the feeling of two burly alphas on both sides of me felt so freaking amazing. Opening my eyes slowly, I realized Sergio was gone and no longer sleeping between my legs.

There was an emptiness there now that I didn't like.

I just wanted to stay in bed all day with Ian and Evan. Suddenly horrified by my thoughts, I scrambled off the bed and fell to the ground on my butt.

"Hmph, what's going on?" groaned Evan, blearily opening his eyes. When he saw me on the ground, he hurried to my side and helped me up.

"Did she fall off the bed?" asked Ian, sounding amused.

"No I didn't," I said, annoyed at Evan helping me up and seeing me butt naked in the light. "Can you both leave, please? It's the morning now."

"Oh," said Evan in surprise, his eyes widening. "I thought you were enjoying our company."

"No!" I said, panicked. I couldn't lose myself and crave to

be with them. My omega instincts were way off today. I had to figure out a plan to escape and not get comfortable with a pack of alphas. "I mean, I did, but it's time for you to leave."

"Okay, okay," said Ian, pulling on his robe. Evan did the same. They both looked confused at my outburst. "Did anything happen?"

"She probably just needs food," grunted Evan, and I rolled my eyes.

"Please just leave," I said, covering my breasts as much as possible and using my other hand to cover my pussy. My body warmed under their gaze, and I was frightened of losing control. They finally left the room after getting an eyeful of my very bare body. Now wide awake, I suddenly felt guilty and sad about suddenly throwing them out of my room.

But I didn't ask to be here. They knew that.

I walked towards the bed, my heart beating hard and wondering if Sergio had left his little gift for me. Peeking under the pillow, I was relieved to see the pill again. Grabbing it, I ducked into the bathroom and took it, brushing my teeth afterward. I hopped into the shower for a quick scrub and got ready for breakfast. I was in a much better mood after taking the heat suppressant pill, and I was grateful for Sergio. Maybe I shouldn't have been mean to his pack. They were nothing but kind to me.

I picked out a short white dress with matching flip-flops, braiding my hair back in two neat cornrows. I looked decent and clean without a ton of makeup on, just a little bit of eyeliner and lipstick. I didn't want to attract too much attention, especially from the creepier alphas.

"Is there something wrong, Olivia?" asked Ian, sliding into the seat next to me as I slowly ate breakfast alone at an isolated table. I didn't really feel like socializing with any of the omegas today, and my heart was pit-pattering in a panic to leave this fucking building.

I wanted out.

"I just really want to leave this place," I said, looking around like a trapped creature. Brett was smirking at me from across the room, and my stomach flipped in disgust. He was so gross to me. "I'm sorry for being rude to you guys."

"It's okay," said Evan, who was sitting on my other side. "You're perfectly fine."

"Where's Sergio?" I asked. I hadn't seen him all morning, and despite my antics, I was missing his company. I wondered where he was.

"He's out on his alpha vacation," said Ian, and my face fell, but I hid it by eating another spoonful of cereal.

"For how long?"

"A week," said Evan.

"Oh," I said. "I was just curious, that's all."

I wasn't sure how much to reveal to them because I wasn't sure if he told them he was leaving heat suppressant pills for omegas. I would have to keep the secret to myself, no matter what.

"Don't worry, we'll provide whatever he provides to you," said Ian quietly without looking at me as he slathered cheese on a bagel. "If you know what I mean."

"I know," I said, relieved. "Thank you."

"If you're feeling cooped up, we can take you out for a walk on the beach," said Evan.

"Are we allowed to go outside?" I asked, shocked. I assumed omegas were supposed to stay cooped up until the end of time.

"Yes," said Evan. "But only if there are alpha handlers present. Would you like to join us?"

"How could I turn that down?" I said, my voice lighting up with hope. "Hell yeah, I want to get out of here."

The two alphas chuckled, and Ian kissed me on the cheek. I smiled, my face growing warm at the contact. I couldn't wait to go outside and feel the sand on my toes. I ate the rest of my breakfast pretty quickly after that, which was not lost on the alphas.

SERGIO

"Hello Henry," I greeted as he walked into my room. He sat on the armchair in front of the flat-screen television, crossing his legs and intertwining his fingers in a businesslike manner.

"Brett has brought up a concern to me," he said. Furrowing my eyebrows, I wondered what the hell Brett needed. "He said you haven't had a chance to bring an omega here, and you could be feeling...a little left out."

"No, I'm fine," I said quickly to dispel any ideas he was coming up in that conniving mind of his.

Henry was the type of alpha who seemed harmless to omegas with the charming personality he displayed in front of them. But behind closed doors, he displayed a cold, calculated manner in how he *really* sees omegas in front of a few choice alphas he deemed his personal favorites.

I wasn't his favorite, and he always questioned why I didn't take more of a part handling omegas or volunteering in the second building where omegas gave birth.

"There is an omega not far from here," he continued to say as if I hadn't interrupted him. "She lives on a farm with her parents, and she's nineteen. Rebecca has long brown hair, tender and a perfect omega to birth our babies."

I had to be careful about how I chose my next words. I

would be killed instantly if Henry suspected I wasn't loyal to him.

"I wouldn't feel bad if another alpha took on this project," I said. "I was really looking forward to visiting my family."

"We all know you don't have family," he countered, eyes flashing.

"My adoptive parents *are* my family," I said, even though I had moved out when I was thirteen after finding out they weren't biologically related to me. However, there was no way Henry could know this information.

"If you're not ready to take on this project and bring us the omega, I will ask you to resign effective immediately," said Henry. "Your choice."

I had seen what happened to the alphas that he fired. To prevent his secret from getting out, the alpha would be found dead the next morning after being tortured. A chill went down my spine at the thought. I also didn't want to risk leaving Olivia here all by herself.

"I can get the omega," I said finally. "Not a problem at all. I just didn't want to miss my vacation time."

"Perfect," he purred with a wide grin. "I will give you an extra week for vacation. Does that sound alright?"

I couldn't leave Olivia for that long.

"I won't be needing it," I said. "I'm happy to take on this project, and I'm glad that you trust me in this."

"Of course I trust you," he said, leaning back in the chair. "You've shown how dedicated you are over all these years. It won't be long before I name you as a chief officer."

"I look forward to that," I said, even though I didn't mean that at all. Maybe I could somehow ditch the assignment he gave me and go into hiding.

"Claws will be joining you on your expedition," said Henry, dispelling all my thoughts of ditching the mission.

"What?"

"He's waiting downstairs for you," he said with a smirk as if he had read my mind. Then he got up from the chair and headed to the door. "Have a fantastic vacation, Sergio."

I nodded curtly, and he finally left.

Looking back at my suitcase, I shook my head in shock at what had happened. I decided to stuff my belongings in a backpack I could easily carry. I couldn't believe he gave me this project. Most alphas would be honored to take it on, but after I saw the true nature of the OBC, I didn't want any part of it. My mission was to take it down, not feed them more omegas to breed.

After I finished packing, I left my room and headed downstairs to greet Claws. He was a big, burly man with a huge beard and a face covered in scars and piercings. He was usually the one designated to kidnap and bring omegas to the OBC. He was fully trained in the art of a smooth kidnapping.

I reluctantly shook his hand.

"Newbie alpha aren't ya'?" he said, crushing my hand.

"Not really," I said. "I just never kidnapped..."

"Don't you worry. I'll teach you the art in no time. You're with the best trainer in town," he said. "Let's go find this damn farm."

A small black car was parked in front of the building, and I got into the passenger seat, thinking of ways to ditch Claws and this mission entirely. For the life of me, I couldn't imagine bringing in a helpless omega to meet her fate.

Claws got into the driver's seat and grabbed a handful of peanuts sitting next to him, crunching the shell and all. My head flew back against the chair as he zoomed down the road.

"Can't you drive a little slower?".

"Fuck no, I could already smell the omega," he said. "Now, stop being a wuss before we even start the mission. Buckle up beta."

"Fuck you," I said.

He chuckled, spitting out a shell out the window as he raced down the road. "Now let me explain what we're going to do. There's duct tape in the back, ropes, and handcuffs if you're feeling in the mood. If you know what I mean..."

Seven

OLIVIA

later that morning, a walk on the beach was everything I needed.

I strolled between Ian and Evan, feeling the sun on my face and the breeze flowing around me, occasionally lifting my dress. The warm sand underneath my feet felt so amazing to me as I walked with the two alphas.

I must have taken freedom for granted. Absorbing the air and the breeze, I was lost to the sounds of the ocean waves crashing against the shore.

The smell of Ian's cologne would waft to me every couple of minutes.

"Whatever cologne you put on smells really nice," I commented, looking over at him. He smiled proudly.

"I collect them," he said.

"There's a shit ton of them in his room," grunted Evan and I giggled. "Hoarder, that one."

"Hey! I like collecting them," said Ian. "By the way, may I hold your hand while we walk?"

"Oh," I said. "Sure."

Evan also offered his hand, and it felt almost natural as they entwined their fingers between mine.

My heart pounded a little faster, and my body felt warmer as we walked.

My hands encircled with their large paws made me feel warm and safe. My little omega heart within me was flipping out, being so close to these alphas. Their pheromones and their scent were clouding my judgment, but I didn't care at this moment. I was so happy to be out of that building.

Looking around, I noticed the second building I'd never stepped foot in.

"What goes on in that building?" I asked, gazing at the tall glass building. It was even fancier than the current building I was staying in.

"You don't want to go in there," said Evan darkly as he gazed at it. "It's where pregnant omegas reside and give birth. It's also where leftover omegas who never go into heat rot in there or for rowdy omegas to get punished."

"Oh damn," I said, my stomach clenching with disgust.

"Older omegas who can't go into heat would be abandoned there," Ian pitched in.

"That sounds terrible," I said, and the alphas nodded in agreement. "Why do you work here if you think it's terrible too?"

I didn't mean for it to sound judgemental, but I was honestly confused.

"I was eighteen when recruited," said Ian. "I was addicted to drugs and no longer lived at home with my parents. My life would've gone down a miserable hole if Henry hadn't recruited me and forced me to stay off drugs."

"But how did you meet Sergio then?"

"I thought this place was my mission," said Ian. "A place to help omegas who couldn't go into heat and to just cuddle them all night long. I didn't think anything sinister or dark was happening."

"Oh," I said, listening intently. It was interesting to hear an alpha's perspective on breeding omegas like cattle and what he thought.

"When I snuck into the Birthing Building and saw the true horrors of what was going on, I met Sergio, who was outside the building taking pictures," he said. "I asked him why the hell he was doing that, and I guess he saw how freaked out I was to trust me with his secret."

"And that's how you joined his pack," I whispered, and he nodded proudly.

"He's a trustworthy alpha and brave as fuck," said Ian in a low voice when we started to see the beach populating with alpha handlers and their omegas.

"I agree," said Evan. "I was friends with Sergio before we both arrived here at the same time. Sergio is the one who found out about this place while searching for his mother, but he never found her."

"Sergio's mom was here?" I asked in shock. It was crazy to me that his own mother had stayed here.

I was starting to see them in a new light. Maybe they weren't as conniving as I thought.

"He believes that's the case," said Evan. "It's the only reason we ended up here. He didn't tell me the specifics, but I was willing to support him as a friend in whatever way he needed."

"That's nice, what you did for him," I said, blinking as the ocean water droplets hit my eyes. "I wish I could see my friends again."

"You will," said Ian, squeezing my hand comfortingly.

"I don't think I ever will," I said, eyes burning with impending tears. Then, in a lower voice, "Do you think you can help me see them again?"

"Let's just say it's in the works," said Evan, kissing my forehead. His kiss was tender and soft, communicating to me that he cared, and my heart thumped in my chest.

"Just don't forget me," I said in a low voice.

"We most definitely won't, and that's a promise," said Ian, and I blushed. I suddenly noticed Brett approaching us, his electric blue hair standing out from the crowd. My heart rate increased, and I slowed down. The alphas noticed this, immediately standing in front of me to block me from Brett's view.

"Don't be scared," Evan quickly said to me, looking back briefly to check if I was okay.

"Brett, what do you need?" asked Ian when he approached. "Clearly, this omega doesn't like you, just like all the other omegas. What did you do to her?"

"Nothing at all," he said in his obnoxious weaselly voice. "You might want to consider sharing her with me. It's not fair you get all the good ones."

Evan growled from deep within his chest, and I could even see the back of his white shirt vibrating from the intensity of his growl.

"Leave, Brett," said Evan.

"You're going to regret it," said Brett, threateningly. He sounded annoyed at the same time, and everything in my body screamed that he was a danger to me. I couldn't see him, but my heart was still racing by the time he walked away from us.

Ian turned first and cupped my chin between his fingers.

"Did Brett ever do anything to you? You can't exactly hide your emotions from us," said Ian.

"His presence, that's all," I said quickly. "I heard bad things."

The tension on his face eased, "Well, he won't dare touch you. And if anything happens, he's dead. But you'll need to tell us if he does."

I nodded, and Evan hugged me.

"You're not like other omegas," said Evan, pulling back and holding me by the shoulders. "I don't want to leave your side even if I just met you. Don't you feel like that about her too, Ian?"

"I mean, I wasn't ready to admit it, but Evan is right," said Ian, and my inner omega self did back flips, excited and overjoyed at the feelings she arose in the alphas. It was a natural response for me. A calling to join a pack that I never felt before.

"I'm glad you like me," I said, twirling a strand of my hair that had come loose. For years, I had fended off asshole alphas, and I was way too afraid to admit my feelings whenever I met a decent one. "Could you both walk me to my room?"

Ian puffed out his chest proudly, and I could feel the alpha pride oozing from them. Alphas naturally felt a need to be the protector and provider for an omega. I wasn't trying to take advantage because I was actually terrified of Brett coming into my room and doing what he did like last time. I was scared to be alone now.

We stopped in front of my room, and the alphas had a hard time leaving me alone.

"Are you sure you're okay?" asked Ian.

"I'm much better now after the walk on the beach," I said.

"There's going to be a dance tomorrow during dinner," said Evan, still holding my hand. "I would love it if you came. It's in the Social Room and redesigned to be a party room."

I sighed heavily. I hated taking part in any of the planned activities.

But I was starting to enjoy spending time with Ian and Evan. And I missed Sergio and his calming presence, which I felt very safe around.

"You look like we invited you to a funeral," said Ian. "It's just a fun gathering. You don't even need to dance."

"Are you *sure*?"

"Yes," chuckled Ian, pushing back his wavy hair, revealing more of his jawbone. His youthful good looks weren't lost on me, and I couldn't help but stare at the thin sideburns on his face. "It's very annoying being surrounded by clingy omegas, so having you would fend off everyone."

"That's not nice," I said, my face falling.

"Hey, I'm kidding," said Ian, rubbing my arm. "Our job is to cuddle omegas, and I enjoy that part, but after spending time with you- you make it so that you're the only omega I want to be around. You're the first and only omega I actually enjoy hanging out with."

"Oh wow," I said breathlessly. His words ignited something deep within me. It was like I wanted to make him even more happier with me. "I enjoy being around you too."

His eyes were on my lips, and my heart pounded wildly the closer he came.

He very gently lifted my face and pressed his warm lips onto mine.

Oh my god, my first kiss.

I allowed my eyes to flutter closed as I stood there, unsure what to do except kiss him back. After a few seconds, my lips naturally molded around his, and my heart rate increased the more he kissed me. My body pressed against his, and I felt Evan coming around behind me, planting kisses on my neck.

Evan's hot lips burned a trail across my collarbone, igniting more flames of desire to rush through my body and coat my pussy. I was throbbing now between my legs as I inhaled Ian's alpha cologne and Evan's woody scent.

Breaking the kiss, I licked my lips and opened my eyes in uncertainty.

"You were my first *real* kiss," I said.

"Damn," said Ian in wonderment, gazing at me with something else in his eyes that I didn't recognize. His glowing eyes were darker and more feral. All I knew was that it made the slick between my legs slide down my thighs while my pussy throbbed even more. "Beat that, Evan."

"Our moment will be special," promised Evan, giving me one last peck on the neck. "But I won't make you wait for long."

Oh fuck.

No matter how hard I tried to avoid having feelings for an alpha pack, it was naturally happening, and I was going to get my heart broken once I found a way out of this camp.

Eight

SERGIO

"Ahh, look at her," said Claws. We were parked a distance from the farmhouse, and we could see the omega deftly unclipping clothes from a line outside of her house. It was obvious she was the omega from the small wolf claw mark on her shoulder. "Look at her long hair and delicate features. She almost makes my cock knot in my pants."

"I'm sure she would appreciate it if you didn't stare at her like she was a piece of meat," I said, disgust rolling over me at the predatory way he gazed at Rebecca. I wondered how the fuck I was going to get out of kidnapping the poor girl who was unaware of two alphas sitting in her front yard.

"This omega will be mine very soon," said Claws. "Her fathers are home and hanging around too much. Might not be the best time for a proper kidnapping."

Thank fuck.

"So when is the best time?"

"We'll stake out the area and wait for her fathers to leave," said Claws. "Then it'll be our chance."

"And if they never leave?"

"Alphas never stay in the house for too long," said Claws. "But if we need to- you can invite them to go hunting, so I can grab the omega."

"Oh hell no," I said, dreading the idea of distracting the fathers just so we could kidnap their daughter.

"It's sunset now," said Claws. "Let's set up camp somewhere, and we'll be back tomorrow morning."

My stomach sank with dread about what the fuck I was going to do. I couldn't refuse, or else Claws would suspect something was up with me. And I couldn't ditch this operation, or I would never be able to get back to the camp.

I would never be able to see Olivia again.

I smiled at the memory of playing puzzles with that omega. Her untamed black hair made my cock wild for her. Her quick-witted responses made me want to hang out with her for hours. I couldn't get enough of her and I never felt that before with anyone else.

And that fact alone scared me to death.

I had vowed never to take on an omega to take advantage of her and for my pack to satisfy their needs with her sexually. But my inner desire was to see her stretched in so many ways that it was impossible to think straight.

I STRETCHED, yawning in the backseat of the car the next morning.

Claws was sleeping outside as per his preference, and I didn't give a fuck as long as I was comfortable.

Or as comfortable as I could make it.

My right shoulder ached from the cramped position I had to sleep in.

Getting out of the car was a struggle because of how fucking stiff my body was, but it was great to get the hell out of the car. I stretched my arms out towards the bright sky, taking in the sounds of the singing birds. Twisting my neck, I looked towards Claws's makeshift tent in the middle of the trees, noticing that it was empty inside.

Looking towards the river, I saw that he was brushing his teeth and wearing a towel around his waist, giving me an enthusiastic wave. I also dipped my hands into the moving river, washing my face briskly. I needed to be alert and awake for whatever Claws was planning to do.

After we were done with our morning ablutions, I got back into the car with Claws, and he drove towards the farmhouse again, which was about five miles from our camp. During the drive, my mind raced with what to do as I clutched the handle of my pistol tucked at my side. A part of me contemplated just allowing it to happen because I'd break the omegas out of the camp anyway, but that wasn't guaranteed. I wasn't even certain if the Royal Pack was working with Henry or not. Because if they weren't, they would have raided the place by now.

We reached the farmhouse, parking a distance away.

"Let's walk the rest of the way and scope out the area," said Claws, licking his lips. "Tonight, she will be mine."

I didn't reply to that; instead, I felt sick to my stomach as we snuck through the trees. We stopped upon seeing the farmhouse, and we were crouching behind shrubbery.

"Looks like no one's home," I said, relieved not to see the omega hanging around outside, ready for the taking.

"No, just wait and see," said Claws, scratching his beard. "Just because her fathers aren't home, doesn't mean she isn't there."

Sure enough, after a couple minutes, the omega walked into clear view, holding a pouch of chicken feed and sprinkling the food on the ground as the chickens gathered around her.

"Her parents could be at home," I warned when Claws started moving in her direction.

"Her fathers' boots are gone if you hadn't noticed," said Claws. "You have a lot to learn, newbie alpha."

"Just because I don't agree with kidnapping doesn't mean I'm no less than an alpha," I growled behind his shoulder as he gazed at the omega.

"Better be careful with your words," muttered Claws darkly. "Or I will need to report you."

I couldn't proceed with kidnapping this omega. It wasn't right.

But suddenly, Claws began to charge towards the omega, sprinting towards her. Before she could even turn to acknowledge him, I gripped the cold metal of my gun.

My heart thumping, I pulled the pistol from the holder and held it up.

Taking aim between his shoulder blades, I pulled the trigger while squeezing one eye shut. Screams rang in the air. Claws's body flopped onto the ground at her feet in slow motion before me. Or that was what it seemed to me.

"Stay calm!" I yelled at the screaming omega and her frantic mother, who had rushed out with an apron tied around her pudgy middle.

"What's going on?" screamed the mother, watching me as I tucked the pistol back into the holder of my jeans.

"I suggest you leave the area right away," I commanded. I lifted the dead body of Claws over my shoulder. *Fuck, he weighed a shit ton*. My knees nearly buckled from the weight of this horrible alpha. "They are coming for your daughter, and they know where you live."

"What?!" said the mother in disbelief.

"What do we do, Mom?" I heard Rebecca saying.

I couldn't listen or engage in conversation with them as I walked to the car while carrying this gigantic alpha on my back. Sweat ran down my back under the hot sun, and his blood was leaving a trail to the car. I had to get the fuck out of here before the omega's fathers returned home from wherever they were. They would follow the trail, and I needed to drive as far as possible before that happened.

I was going to be in so much fucking trouble. To kill an alpha was punishable by death, except for good reason. But if an alpha killed another alpha, there could be a trial. As I dumped the body into the trunk of the car, I wanted to vomit, seeing his look of permanent shock and blood seeping from his chest. I had never in my life killed another soul before.

Fuck. Fuck. Fuck.

With shaking fingers, I dug into his pockets for the car keys while holding my breath to block the odor of his body. Then I slammed the trunk shut, immediately hopping into the driver's seat. *I had to get out here.* That was all I was thinking about. Turning the key into the ignition, I zoomed the fuck out of there and into any random direction on the road.

There was a dead alpha in my trunk from the most notorious breeding camps on Howl's Edge.

And I had no idea what the hell I was going to do now.

Nine

OLIVIA

Oh, this pedicure was lovely.

I relaxed back in the cushioned chair as the beta workers in their trim yellow uniforms massaged my feet in the warm tub of water. The spa was crowded with omegas getting ready for the dance today. I didn't realize it was a big deal until Julie invited me to come to the spa.

"I'm not feeling so well," complained Treasure, with her hand on her forehead. I looked over to my right and saw her dainty features twisted in pain.

Uh, uh. She could be nearing heat.

I suddenly felt guilty that I had help with heat suppressant pills while she had none. But there was really nothing I could do about it, even though I wanted to save every omega in here.

"Is it something you ate?" asked her older sister, who was sitting to my left. She had a face mask on and slices of cucumber over her eyes as she relaxed in her chair.

"No," moaned Treasure, shutting her eyes tight. "The headache just passed. I felt a weakness through my body that I can't explain."

"Do you think it's your heat?" asked Julie.

"I really hope so," said Treasure, to my shock. "I really like Rodmon and his pack. They might be the alphas of my dreams. I don't think having a baby with them would be too bad."

Wait, didn't they know the babies would get taken away? And who knew what happened to the omegas afterward?

"I...hope not," said Julie worriedly as she plucked off the cucumbers covering her eyes. She looked at me with stark panic in her eyes.

"Didn't you say this was way better than your past life?" I reminded her. Julie had told me about her narcissistic mother and how she was happy to escape her. And that this place would take care of them.

"I had never seen the other building, but the omegas say good things about it," said Julie, with doubt in her voice. I wished to tell them what it was really all about, but there was no use scaring them when there wasn't a way out. It was better to have Treasure excited about it all than dreading it and ruining her night.

After the spa treatment, we joined all the other omegas in a vast dressing room that had rows of fancy dresses hung in neat rows as beta workers scrambled about grabbing different sizes for the omegas once they stated their size.

"I have no idea what I want to wear," I said, trying to take in all the different sparkly dresses. I sifted through the dresses and finally found one that caught my eye. Pulling it off the rack, I admired the silver sequins on the strapless sky-blue dress. The front portion was covered in sequins, and it flowed gracefully from the waist.

"That's beautiful," said Julie over the sound of the females in the background and chatter of excitement. This was like an omega's paradise. Spas, dressing up, and dancing with alphas.

"That dress is beautiful, too," I said, admiring the glittering red dress she was holding up.

"It's nice, but it's a bit much," she said, biting her lip.

"Oh, come on," I huffed, looking around at all the omegas who had piles of makeup on their faces and were wearing the loudest, outrageous dresses. "We chose the tamest dresses compared to what they're wearing. Don't worry about it, and have fun."

"What?" she said, smiling. "You were the pessimist one when you got here."

"Well...not anymore," I said. The truth was that I was looking forward to spending another cuddling session with Ian and Evan tonight. Last night, we had a lot of fun laughing and finishing up the puzzle game late into the night. "I'm going to try on this dress. See you in a bit."

Going into one of the smaller individual dressing room stalls, I closed the door behind me and removed my black shirt and leggings. I had grabbed some shapewear to help with my tummy on the way here, so I quickly pulled it up over my thighs, slimming me down before I put the dress on. I was self-conscious about my weight since I enjoyed food outings a whole lot with my family. When things got too out of control, I'd diet for a week and then back to my normal eating pattern the week after. My belly wasn't too noticeable, but with a tight dress on, I felt more self-conscious than usual.

When I put the dress on, I gasped as I looked at the mirror. The sky-blue dress flattered my curves and hid all the areas I didn't want to show. It flared at my hips just like I thought it would, the fabric lightly brushing against my ankles. I couldn't wait for Evan and Ian to see me in this dress. I adjusted the chest area to cover up some of my cleavage, but my ample breasts weren't going to be tamed. Sighing, I gave up but decided that this was the perfect dress for me.

I walked out of the fitting room, and Julie's eyes widened upon seeing me in the dress and at my cleavage.

"You were hiding those away until now," she said, narrowing her eyes in jealousy, and I laughed.

"No I wasn't," I said. "I just wear big shirts, that's all. And I'm too shy."

"Don't be shy today, girl. Today's your time to show off," said Julie, touching the fabric of the dress. "By the way, this dress is simply gorgeous on you. I'm sure you think so, too."

"I do," I said, smiling. "I need to get my hair and makeup in order. The dress is the hardest part."

"Ahh! I'm so excited to change, too," said Julie, slinging the red dress over one arm. "I'll see you at the dance if I don't find you."

∼

BEFORE WE COULD ENTER the Social Room, I was standing in line behind all the other omegas, with Julie standing behind me. I peeked through the glass windows, seeing the front of the line where Henry stood inside the room dressed in a sleek black suit with a red tie.

Every omega gave him her hand, and he would kiss their hand in greeting. Then, there would be alphas in a separate line behind him, ready to take the omega to the dance floor.

The room wasn't filled with cushions on the ground tonight. Instead, there were pink, purple, and blue lights dancing around the huge room, which had been cleaned out for the dance.

There was a table full of refreshments, and everywhere around me was the air of excitement, along with loud chatter surrounding me. The omegas were excited, and I could smell it in their excessive perfuming. I was only excited to see Ian and Evan again. Last night's cuddling session had turned me on so much since I did nothing but kiss Ian most of the time while Evan spooned me from behind.

"I can't wait to get inside," said Treasure. I could smell her perfume the strongest. Her omega scent smelled like cotton candy. I hoped she was ready and prepared for when she would go into heat because it seemed like her heat would happen in a matter of hours. Her face was flushed pink, and the tendrils of her blond hair stuck to her sweaty forehead. I could see her wild eyes scanning through the glass window, searching for the particular alpha she had talked about all day at the spa.

Once we were inside the Social Room, it was finally my turn to greet Henry.

"Thank you for hosting this," I said, copying all the other omegas who went ahead of me in line. They had said the same creepy phrase, and I decided to do the same so I didn't stand out like a sore thumb.

"You are welcome," he said in that robotic voice of his. He kissed my hand and smiled at me. "You look particularly scrumptious."

My heart beat faster with nervousness. I hadn't heard him say that to the other omegas.

I turned, seeing Ian and Evan appear out of nowhere as they grabbed my hands in both of theirs. I was relieved to be pulled out from there, but being around Henry made me uneasy.

Once we were out of the crowd, I sighed in relief, and they released my hands, giving me a once-over with their dark gazes.

"You are shining tonight," said Evan, appraising me with his gaze. My face burned, but I smiled shyly. I had never dressed up like this to the fullest.

"I don't know how I'll last tonight without knotting your pretty pussy," said Ian.

"Oh my god, Ian, ew," I exclaimed, and he chuckled, straightening the tie around his neck as if it was too tight. We had come close to knotting several times last night while cuddling.

"Your breasts, my god," he said. "I absolutely can't wait to rip it off from you tonight."

My chest rose as my breathing quickened, giving him an even clearer view of my breasts.

"Fuck," said Evan. "Dance with me first."

"Sure," I said as Ian grumbled in annoyance. Evan took me by the arm, leading me to the dance floor as Ian went to grab a drink. The room was dark except for the lights flashing around the dance floor.

His hand snaked around my waist, pulling me to him as we slow-danced in circles, matching the other couples who were dancing in threes and some even in fours. The feeling of Evan's strong body pressed against mine made me throb like crazy between my legs. I wanted him despite the protests in my brain. His short, wavy hair covered half his eyes, giving him a sultry look that made my heart tremble.

"Do the omegas go crazy over you during cuddle sessions?" I asked. I felt just a tiny bit jealous that these alphas had to cuddle with other omegas, even though they've only cuddled me for the past few nights.

"Some do," he answered gruffly. Then he tilted his head in a knowing look as he gazed into my face. "But I'm a professional, and I've never kissed an omega here."

No matter how steamy things got last night between Ian and me, he never once tried to kiss me on the lips, so I believed him. We came close a few times, but he would pull back, leaving me to wonder.

"Why not?" I asked.

"Because kisses are powerful," he said. "Once an omega

goes into heat and you never see her again, the heartbreak after that is ten times worse if you've built that type of connection. If I kissed you...I will never let you go."

Ten

OLIVIA

Dancing with Ian was light and easy as Evan's words replayed in my brain. He didn't play around when it came to omega's feelings, and I appreciated that about him. But I wondered how much of that was true.

"Has Evan ever kissed omegas here?" I asked Ian, giving him a look to tell me the truth. It's not that I didn't believe Evan, but an alpha male that hot should have at least enjoyed a couple of kisses.

"I haven't seen him get all crazy to kiss so fast. He takes his time, why?" asked Ian, deftly spinning me around the dance floor. He was swift on his feet and seemed to know what he was doing when it came to dancing, unlike myself. With Evan, we moved slowly to not mess up, and we bonded over the fact that we both sucked at dancing.

"I was just curious, that's all," I said.

"It means that he doesn't want to break your heart," explained Ian. "Don't overthink it."

When he dipped me during the dance, he lowered his lips to mine, and my heart rate sped up. He kissed me like that, holding my lips for a full thirty seconds before releasing me.

When I straightened back up, I was breathless and a little dizzy doing that while dancing.

"And you're an expert at kissing," I accused, narrowing my eyes jokingly.

"Not at all," he said with a smirk, leading me away from the dance floor and towards the long dinner table piled with different varieties of food. I was impressed as I took in the mini-cakes, a small fillet, rice, and salad set up neatly in front of each chair placement, exactly for the same number of people here at the dance. I wondered what happened to the leftovers if someone wanted to skip dinner.

But I was definitely not one to waste my food.

Taking a bite from the steak, my mouth watered for more right away. It was so tender and burst in flavors on my tongue. I quickly dug in without hesitation, hungry from all the dancing.

"Thank you all for coming," announced Henry after ringing a glass cup with a silver spoon for everyone's attention. Brett was sitting beside him with a permanent smirk on his face, watching the omegas with hawk eyes like he always tended to do. When his gaze fell on me, I looked down, shrinking down in my seat.

"What's wrong, Livvy?" asked Ian, touching my shoulder. "I can smell your scent changing."

"Nothing," I said, hushing him so we could listen to Henry's speech.

"I encourage you all to stay unified in our mission to create the strongest nation Howl's Edge has ever known," said Henry to loud clapping and cheers from everyone. "That is all I have. You can go back to celebrating our mission."

Great. The mission is to get knotted and have babies for these alphas.

"Ian," I said, finishing up my plate and wiping my mouth with the handkerchief.

"Yes?"

"Thank you for giving me a chance at life," I said in a low voice. "You know..."

He blinked quickly to show that he understood.

"You're welcome. But please don't mention it anymore."

I nodded, taking a sip of water. "I need to get out of this stuffy room."

"Me too," said Ian.

We both looked over at Evan, who had finished his plate already and was digging into the large slice of cake in front of him.

"Evan, are you done eating yet? We're leaving, man," said Ian.

"Give me a minute," Evan said, and I smiled at how he closed his eyes in delight while eating. "We're not all like you. I love a good dessert to motivate me during my workout sessions."

"It must be hard to keep up with the way you look," I said, giggling when Evan fed me a spoonful of cake. It felt like a kiss in a way since his lips had touched the same spoon. The moisture of the spoon, made my center throb at the intimacy. "Mhm, that's some good cake."

"I can grab a full slice of cake for you," said Ian, sounding slightly pissed off that Evan one-upped him in the romance department.

"It's okay. It tastes even better sharing," I said when Evan pulled me onto his lap to feed me another bite. I leaned against his chest, allowing my mouth to fall open when he fed me another spoonful.

"You know it does," Evan grunted in my ear, and I clenched my thighs together when his rumbling voice caused my body to tremble. He pressed his lips to my ear, quietly nibbling my earlobe as he fed me more cake. "She finished my slice. Ian, feed her some more."

I sighed, rolling my head to the side to give Evan access to my neck as Ian deftly grabbed a spoon and another slice of cake, feeding me while Evan kissed my neck. I swallowed the cake, growing self-conscious about doing this in public. But upon looking around, I saw a lot of omegas and alphas were in far more lewd positions right in front of everyone.

"Do you like the cake, little omega?" asked Evan.

"It's so sweet and delicious," I moaned as his lips pressed with more urgency across my neck, nearer to my lips now. I craved for his lips to touch mine. I could feel his cock underneath my ass getting harder as I wiggled over him. When I closed my eyes to savor the next bite, I felt his lips slide over mine. And I nearly gasped in shock, feeling him kiss me, but I kept my eyes closed to not ruin the kiss.

"I had to taste what you were tasting," growled Evan, breaking the kiss. I opened my eyes and smiled.

"Of course," I said sarcastically. Deep down, I was thrilled that he'd wanted to kiss me, but I hoped I wasn't being naive or dumb that he chose me out of all omegas. I'm sure he had kissed others before me, and I had to keep that in my mind so I didn't get too excited.

"Do you want more cake, sweetheart? Or did Evan's kiss ruin it all?" asked Ian.

"I'm full, Ian, thank you," I said, and he nodded, shoving the plate away.

"Fuck," groaned Evan when I moved a little to get off his lap and his hard cock. "I want you to sit on me forever. Even better, I want you to sit on my face later tonight."

Slick seeped down to my inner thighs, a reminder of my omega need, and my pussy throbbed at his request.

"Let's...let's go outside now," I said breathlessly. "I need some air."

"Definitely," said Ian, offering his hand and helping me off of Evan's lap. "A nice walk on the beach under the moon sounds very relaxing, doesn't it?"

Still breathing hard from Evan's attentions, I walked between them, holding their hands as we walked to the exit of the ballroom.

The tingling feeling between my legs grew more and more insistent.

I couldn't forget Evan's kisses on my neck and his hard cock under my butt. I wanted him just as badly, but I had to calm down. Maybe the walk on the beach would calm me down. Especially after being in a room trapped with alphas' strong scents overwhelming the light, flowery scents of omegas flitting about. I leaned on Ian's arm as we walked since my feet ached from the high heels. I've never worn heels for so long like this, and I hated them. I couldn't wait to fling them off once we got to the sand outside.

"Oh, leaving already?" asked Henry, who was standing at the door and chatting away with a couple of alphas. They looked at us as we prepared to leave.

"Yes, sir," said Ian.

Then Henry turned to me, "Have you been enjoying yourself, Olivia?"

How the heck did he remember my name? Unless he had a super great memory and memorized all the omegas.

"I did, thank you for asking," I said, eager to leave with my alphas and enjoy the rest of our night cuddling.

"Where are you planning on going right now?"

"Just a walk down the beach," I said, smiling politely at him. I was scared to show any rudeness to him, or else I could easily lose these alphas.

"That sounds delightful," said Henry. "Tonight, I will be your handler along with Ian here. Evan, you will need to sit this one out."

What?! I didn't have the slightest attraction to Henry, and I was looking forward to Evan tonight.

"Wait, no," growled Evan, and Henry flashed him a look. "I'm on the schedule tonight with Olivia."

"Aw, I hope you're not getting attached," said Henry, clapping him on the arm. "Consider this an off day. I can make and change the schedules at my leisure. You know this."

Evan, breathing heavily- stormed out of the ballroom, slamming the double doors wide open. Oh my god, he must have really been wanting to spend the night with me just as I looked forward to spending it with him.

"I hope you're not offended by this change of plan, Olivia," said Henry with a sickly sweet smile, rubbing a hand through his slicked-back hair as if he didn't just piss off a large alpha, and taking his omega for the night.

Yes, I was considering myself as *his* in my mind. I was for Sergio, Ian, and Evan even if they hadn't acknowledged it yet. The heat between us was electrical, and I missed Sergio's gentle smile. Or maybe I was starting to get brainwashed, but I was really starting to get attached, and my stomach hurt at the thought of spending any part of the night with Henry.

"Not at all," I said, my heart racing. "I would love to spend tonight with you, sir."

"Good girl," said Henry, pulling my hand in his and kissing it. "I will meet you in your bedroom during the cuddle session. No need to stay up if you're tired."

There was no way in hell I was going to fall asleep before he got into the bed with me.

"Okay," I said, my voice small as Ian squeezed my other hand in comfort.

I didn't like this at all, and there had to be some reason Henry felt the need to be with me tonight.

Eleven

SERGIO

Thwack.

Sweat poured down my face as I shoveled piles of rock to bury the dead alpha.

It was a muggy night, and my hands were torn from the damn shovel. But I would heal quickly- one of the perks of being an alpha werewolf. Dropping the shovel, I walked to the trunk of the car and opened it. The foul odor of Claws wafted around me as I threw his dead body over my shoulders in the dead of night.

It wasn't a great feeling, knowing I had a dead body in the car for hours. I had driven as far out as I could away from the farm.

"There you go, mother fucker," I said, dumping him in the shallow grave. I didn't bother to make it any deeper. I just had to get rid of him because I only had days to get my original mission done.

My mission was to free the omegas trapped at the OBC.

Claws lay prone in his grave, his milky eyes staring straight at me in the dark and giving me the shivers, so I quickly poured the dirt and rocks over his head first, following the rest of his body.

Once I was finished, I peeled off my blood-stained shirt and pants, washing them in the flowing river. I had to find my way back into the city. From there, I could get a new supply of heat suppressant pills and present my evidence of mistreatment of omegas to the Royal Pack. I couldn't wait to get this all done so I could see Olivia's angelic face again. If the Royal Pack weren't going to help, then I would break her out myself.

Hanging my wet clothes off the back seat of the car, I sat in the driver's seat, only wearing my briefs.

I needed to get as far away from here as possible. Starting the car, I zoomed down the dirt path, leaving the buried body of the alpha behind me.

~

Olivia

"Just sleep, it's okay," comforted Ian while holding me in the bed while I fretted.

"I can't until he's here," I said, pressing my nose into his chest as I waited for Henry to join us in the bed. The uncertainty of what to expect was killing me.

Did Henry talk in his sleep? Was he gentle or rough?

I needed to know everything before I could drift off into blissful sleep. In my earlier days of being here, I had run on no sleep, not knowing any of the alphas. And by the morning came, I kicked the alphas out as early as possible so I could at least get an hour's worth of sleep.

"Don't worry, I won't let anything happen to you," said Ian, kissing my forehead. I couldn't even relax enough to make out with Ian. We skipped the walk on the beach since Evan had disappeared, and we decided instead to stay in my room to talk until Henry showed up.

Just then, I heard the room door open, and my heart pounded fast. Ian held me tighter, sensing my fear.

"Why hello again, Olivia," said Henry in a smooth-as-honey voice that sent chills down my back. He pulled the sheets back and slid in behind me, pressing his naked body against mine.

"Hi," I said meekly to show that I was awake in case he had other frightening ideas. Then he started to hump me from behind, and my eyes widened. Ian, sensing my shock, lifted his head.

"Henry, is that necessary?"

"Ian, I need you to do the same thing," ordered Henry. Then, in a calmer tone, near my ear, "Why haven't you gone into heat yet, little omega?"

"I don't know," I stuttered, trying to close my eyes, but I was shocked.

I could feel his slim body pressing up against mine as he humped me, his dick slapping against my ass but not going inside. Ian was gently rubbing his body against mine, pressing his cock against the outside of my pussy.

"This is how your handlers should be treating you," whispered Henry. "Is this what they were doing to you or not?"

"Sort of."

"Then you should have gone into heat by now," said Henry while Ian stayed awfully quiet. I was scared to death of Henry discovering that I took heat suppressant pills, so I nodded in agreement. His body against mine was having an effect on me that I couldn't control.

My pussy was throbbing between the two male bodies, and warmth was starting to grow between my legs. The flares of the heat would stop right at my abdomen, and I knew that was the heat suppressant pills helping me.

"Oh," I said when I felt a little bit of a pang go through my belly.

"I help out when I feel that an omega is struggling," said Henry. "I apologize that the alpha handlers aren't equipped with emergency techniques like this. They are not patient."

"It's...it's okay," I said, trying to even my breathing. My heart rate was rapidly increasing against my will, and I couldn't seem to control my body's responses while Henry was trying to force my heat to emerge.

"Close your eyes," said Henry while rubbing my belly and breathing against my neck. I obeyed and closed my eyes. "Did you ever dream of being a mother one day? To have a little one of your own that looks like an exact copy of you?"

"Um."

"Answer me, omega, and be truthful."

An image of a little boy with curly black hair floated in my mind, and tears sprung to my eyes. I wanted to hold him so badly, but I wanted to be secure with a pack of alphas that I loved first.

"I do, but I want to be loved first."

"You are loved here, my dear," said Henry in that creepy voice of his, but I deemed his words to be untrue. "Every alpha who cuddles you loves you. Do you ever imagine your belly growing and the baby kicking inside you?"

My heart rate increased even more as Henry rubbed my belly in circles while Ian's thighs and chest rubbed over mine. My pulse was racing from arousal and also fear as I felt tendrils of heat spiking through my abdomen.

"Yes," I said, hoping he would stop. I didn't want to go into heat here. I had to fight it. "But wouldn't I lose my baby after giving birth here? Don't you just take them?"

Suddenly, Henry stopped his movements behind me and released his hold on my belly.

"Who told you this information?" he asks, not moving a muscle, but I could hear the stark anger in his voice and Ian's sharp intake of breath.

I knew Ian was worried about me by the way he caressed my arms.

"My cousin Lacy said that could happen before...before she left," I said, realizing I made a horrible mistake. I hoped he wouldn't pin it down to Ian or Sergio saying anything to me.

"She has been lying to you," said Henry, calming down and continuing to rub my belly and press his body against me. "She wasn't meant to be in an omega paradise like this one that I had provided for all omegas. You will be able to have your babies and raise them with the choice of alphas that you love. I make the rules here, and you will have that, Olivia."

My stomach twisted in disgust. It sounded so amazing, but every word he said was a complete lie. I didn't look at Ian, but I could sniff his scent, getting stronger with disapproval. Ian knew that Henry was full of shit. I knew it too, so I couldn't allow my body to be taken by heat.

Closing my eyes, I imagined babies being ripped away from their mothers, and suddenly, the tendrils of heat started to slowly dissipate.

Fuck, it was working.

Shutting my eyes tighter, I imagined crying babies and the horror of the omega mothers here. My body naturally knew it wasn't safe to go into heat, regardless of all the omega pampering they did here and treating me like a queen.

"Do you feel it, my dear? Do you feel the heat in your belly growing?"

"Yes," I moaned, trying to convince him. "I can't believe it."

"Of course," he said in a pleased voice. "You can thank me later when you're pregnant with your child."

Ian held my gaze, and I bit my lip, showing him that I was completely lying to Henry about going into heat, and a look of relief came over his eyes.

Ian kissed me on the cheek, and I smiled.

"Kiss her on the lips, pup," ordered Henry. "If she's letting you kiss her, you might as well kiss her on the lips. I've watched you two on camera, so don't be shy because I'm here."

Ian didn't even spare a glance at the director of the camp as he slowly dipped his head, kissing me squarely on the lips. I closed my eyes, letting my mind float into the safe space with him. His kiss soothed my fears and worries, reminding me of the feelings he held for me. Seagulls and the blue sky filled my mind as I imagined us there as a couple, enjoying ourselves.

When the kiss ended, we looked at each other, and I caressed his soft hair, pushing it back from his sculptured face. I closed my eyes, imagining that it was only Ian with me in bed and not Henry.

"Go to sleep," whispered Ian, and Henry stopped humping against me from behind to allow me to rest.

"Yes, get some rest," said Henry. "By tomorrow morning or afternoon, you will hopefully be in full heat. I can sense you're in pre-heat now."

I closed my eyes, awake for several minutes, listening to Henry snoring behind me while his body was still pressed to mine. Ian's eyes were on me as we gazed at each other in the dark, only slivers of his face showing in the moonlight streaming from the window. He gave me one more peck on the lips, and I smiled softly. Oh, how I wished we were kissing under different circumstances.

"Goodnight, babe," whispered Ian. "Hopefully, he'll be gone before you wake up tomorrow."

I didn't dare reply in case Henry was faking sleep. He didn't seem like he was dumb at all, and I wasn't risking anything. I gave Ian a warning look. "Goodnight, Ian, sleep tight. It was a fun dance, and I'm glad you invited me."

"You looked gorgeous," he said. "I will show Sergio our pictures when he gets back. Just think of that before you sleep."

Twelve

OLIVIA

With my eyes still closed the next morning, I was curled into fetal position on the bed. I listened for heavy breathing behind me, remembering that Henry was my handler for the night, and I didn't want to face him just yet. But upon not hearing anything, I opened my eyes and rubbed the sleep out of my eyes.

No Ian or Henry in the bed.

Panicking that I might go into heat soon like Henry said, I lifted my pillow and saw the beautiful heat suppressant pill lying in wait for me. I picked it up, relieved that Ian had remembered. I was really starting to develop feelings for him, and that freaked me out as much as the thought of going into heat.

"What is that in your hand?" said a voice from a dark corner of the room. Henry was dressed in a white bathrobe with a gold sash on the front.

Oh my god, Henry was still in the room.

I was such a dumbass for not looking around. But I never made smart decisions at eight a.m. in the morning.

"What do you mean?" I asked, trying to play coy while crossing my hands behind my back.

"In your hand," he growled, stalking over to me, and I quickly threw the pill behind me, hoping it would get lost. But he was swift, rushing past me and flipping over the bed. The frame crashed against the wall, and I flinched.

I started to back away in the opposite direction when he picked up the heat suppressant pill. He slowly turned to me, his jaw tight with anger.

"What?" I asked, trying to sound innocent.

"Who gave this to you?" he asked.

"No one."

"Do *not* lie to me, omega."

My heart raced, and my knees trembled as I stood naked before him. I couldn't get the alphas in trouble. They did nothing wrong at all.

"I snuck it in," I said, looking down so he didn't see the lie in my eyes. "I couldn't get rid of it because I'm so scared of getting pregnant, but I'm very happy to be here."

He was quiet for a few minutes, and I slowly looked up to see what he was planning on doing.

"I understand your fear," he said slowly. "But this is a grave offense. You are an omega who refuses to do her duties."

"It'll never happen again, I swear."

"Unfortunately, you need to go into corrections," he said. "Put on your clothes while I make the arrangements."

Fuck my life. I was shaking pretty badly as I heard him talking on his walkie-talkie in a grim voice. He was furious as he explained what had happened in a low voice. I scrambled to put on leggings and a shirt. Using the bathroom while he was busy, I brushed my teeth and combed out my unruly hair, shaking with fear. I had no idea what was going to happen to me once I stepped out of this bathroom.

I wanted to stay in the bathroom for as long as possible but realized I couldn't hide in there forever.

I had to know what Henry had planned for me. Taking a deep breath, I left the bathroom and walked back into the room. Someone else had joined Henry in the room, and I gasped upon seeing who it was.

Brett with his electric blue hair. He looked at me with a knowing smirk as Henry gazed upon me in disapproval.

"Olivia, meet Brett," said Henry. "Because of your disobedience and disloyalty to me, you will be taken to the Birthing Building while Brett brings you to heat using stricter measures."

"What?" I said, nervous butterflies in my stomach. I felt like throwing up at the news, and my breaths turned shallower. "I promise it won't happen again!"

"This is for your benefit," said Henry. "You will become a better omega for your future alphas, and you will thank me for it. You will know what it means to be a true omega. Brett will take you to your nest now."

"Anyone but Brett," I pleaded. "He hurt me."

Henry blinked and pursed his lips.

"She's lying," said Brett. "I was never her handler."

"I'm not lying!"

"Olivia, nothing will save you from this decision," said Henry. "You will also learn when an alpha has made his decision. An alpha never goes back on his word."

I ran to the door, but Brett rushed towards me in a flash. In seconds, he was behind me, gripping my wrists behind my back.

"You will be my new omega," Brett whispered in my ear, and I shivered while struggling to pull away from his grip.

"Brett, don't be creepy," said Henry. "Enjoy yourself, Olivia, and maybe you will have learned a lesson once you are pregnant."

Dread settled in my soul as Brett marched me down the stairs. I struggled to pull away from Brett while screaming. And he twisted my arm so I would stop screaming.

"That hurts!" I said.

"Then shut the fuck up," he growled. "The other omegas will get scared."

"As they should," I said in a normal tone, trying to ease the pressure on my stinging arm. Out of all alphas, Henry had to pick *him* to be my handler?! Brett continued to march me down the stairs, with Henry following close behind us. "Can I at least grab some clothes?"

"You won't need any clothes in omega jail," said Brett with a soft chuckle.

Oh god.

"Hey! What the fuck are you doing with her?" shouted Ian, who was hanging out in the lobby. He stood in front of me, touching my face with concern, and I naturally leaned into the warmth of his hand.

"They're taking me to the other building," I said.

"You can't take her there," Ian yelled in Brett's face, trying to untangle Brett's hands from mine.

"Ian," barked Henry. "Stay back. This omega is dangerous and will be contained until she's ready to mingle again. I will assign you a new omega, so there's no need to worry."

"I don't need a new omega," growled Ian. "Please give her another chance. What the hell did she do?"

"Go ahead, Brett," said Henry, motioning for him to take me out of the building. "Ian, move out of the way."

I watched Ian look down and reluctantly move out of the way while his jaw clenched. His chest puffed with anger, and he gave me a look that he wasn't letting this go.

"Fine," said Ian.

"That's a good kid. Why don't you entertain the omegas upstairs?"

I didn't hear his answer as Brett walked me out into the sun, walking fast-paced towards the Birthing Building. The sand seeped through the slippers and between my toes. I tried to pay more attention to the feeling of that before I was locked up.

"Brett, you don't have to do this," I said, longing to run away and swim in the ocean. "You can be a better alpha."

"This is the best form of alpha I can be," he said, sounding fully convinced in his statement. "Let's go inside."

As we walked into the building, I immediately heard screams and babies crying coming from the top floor. This building looked similar to the other one, with the spiraling staircase and many floors and with a fancy lobby in the front.

"Where are you taking me?" I asked in alarm when he started to take me towards a door marked as 'caution'.

"You won't be hanging upstairs with the omegas giving birth," he said. "You'll be living down here."

I looked down the long flight of stairs that seemed to lead down a huge basement. The screaming sounds upstairs were muted when he closed the basement door.

My heart pounding hard, I walked carefully down the steps, trying to maintain my balance while Brett tried to rush me down. It became darker and darker the more we descended down the basement. We came upon a dark hallway lit up with candles on the walls, and we took a sharp right. Then he pushed me into a room, and I fell forward as he slammed the door shut.

I couldn't see anything in the dark, especially after being out in the sun a few moments ago.

After a couple of seconds for my eyes to adjust, I made out a circular black cushion in the middle of the room. The room was completely bare and chilly except for the lone cushion that was omega-sized.

Was this the pitiful *nest* that Henry was talking about?

The room was cold, and I shivered, crossing my arms over my chest. Brett leaned up behind me, and I recoiled in disgust when I felt his hot breath on my neck.

"Let's get you over to your little nest," he crooned, grabbing me by the arm and sitting me down on his lap on the cushion. I've never been so fearful in my life until now. This was the most scared I had ever been in my life besides getting kidnapped. Brett wasn't an easy alpha, and I knew what he was capable of.

"Brett, please let me go," I said, and he growled until I could feel the tremor down my back.

"Say it one more time, and I'll knot you right now," he said, and I pressed my lips together. I was completely under his mercy right now. He laid his hand on top of tightly clenched thighs. Then he began purring, pressing his mouth against my neck.

I knew what he was doing, but I refused to calm down.

But I was no match for an alpha's purr that could instantly calm an omega. The vibrational waves went through every bone in my body, powerful and seductive. Despite my hate for Brett, he prodded my thighs to open, and I couldn't resist. He squeezed my inner thigh, pushing his hand further up to my trembling pussy.

"I missed your scent," Brett grunted. "I want your scent spilled all over my hand so I can smell you all day long. Your beautiful, naughty cherry scent."

"I'm not naughty or sexy at all," I said, breathing hard as he curled his finger over my pubic bone, cupping my pussy.

"Your pussy says otherwise. She's hot and needy for me. Is that true?"

"No," I said, not wanting to give in to him at all despite my arousal. He made every inch of my skin crawl.

"Admit it," he growled, nipping my neck and I yelped.

"Yes," I said.

"Yes, what, my omega?"

"My pussy is hot and needy for you," I gritted out as if it was painful to say it. But Brett was intense, and I was scared of what he would do if he got angry with me.

"Good girl," he said, squeezing my pussy over my leggings. Then he suddenly ripped the middle of my leggings with his hands, exposing my bare pussy.

Thirteen

OLIVIA

"Oh shit," I moaned as he toyed with my bare clitoris while sitting on his lap. Brett then deposited me onto the cushion on my back and spread my legs out further, using his hands to rip a larger hole into my leggings.

"Ahh, that's perfect," he grunted, kneeling between my legs and staring at his handiwork. I looked up at the ceiling as he touched the folds of my pussy, spreading me open before him. I couldn't look at his face as he sniffed me between my pussy lips. And when I felt his tongue shoot out and lick my clit, my hips jerked. "I missed your taste, sweet thing. Why have you been resisting me this entire time?"

"Because I don't want you. You psychopath!" I said, desperately wanting to kick him in the face as he licked my pussy. I shut my eyes tight, frozen, as I felt his tongue pressing against my clit. He laughed softly at my insult, and it sounded like he was proud of being called a psycho. My thighs shook as he forced an orgasm from me. "Why are you like this? Don't you want an omega to like you?"

"Yummy," he said, slurping and licking all the slick I

released. "I'm going to bring you to heat, even if you took all the heat suppressants. Don't worry, omega."

"I'm not worrying," I said, watching as he sat up, licking his lips. Then he dipped his head one more time between my legs, rubbing his nose across my slick. I lay there frozen, simply watching him.

"I want to smell you before I come back tonight," he said. I breathed a sigh of relief that he wouldn't be here all day. He took one more giant sniff of my pussy and stood up, straightening his black shirt. "Be a good omega. I'll be back for you tonight."

He kissed my inner thigh and finally stood up to leave.

"How long am I going to be in here?!" I shouted, but he ignored my question.

Once he left the room, I was a trembling mess in the middle of the cushion. I slowly sat up and looked at the loose threads from the hole in my leggings, forever exposing my pussy to him. Sitting cross-legged, I ripped the threads off, trying to block off what happened, and instead focused on this single task before me. I sat there for a moment, unsure of what to do. This room was small and claustrophobic, which I hated. And I hated the darkness of it, too, but my eyes were slowly adjusting.

Breathing hard, I stood on shaky legs. There was nothing in this room to look at, no window, no bathroom. Suddenly, my stomach growled for breakfast, and I wondered if someone was going to bring food to me.

I made my way to the door certain that it was locked. But when I twisted the doorknob, I was surprised to find that it was open. Looking outside the door, I didn't see Brett around, so I stood in the carpeted hallway. The flickers of the candles danced around me on the dark purple walls. It was so drab down here, and it felt like an ancient corridor. Quietly walking back up towards the stairs, I decided to try my luck.

When I reached the top of the stairs, I was breathless, and I wanted to scream when I couldn't twist the doorknob open at all.

Shit.

No matter how hard I tried to twist the doorknob, it was locked, and I didn't have a single hair clip on me to try to unlock the door on my own. Starting the slow descent down the stairs, I wondered if it was even possible to escape this damn camp. Outside the buildings, I remembered that there were tons of guards everywhere, and it seemed impossible that any omega would be able to escape. My mind wandered to Lacy, and I wondered if she'd really been able to get away. There was no way of getting information around here, and my imagination was my biggest enemy.

I decided to explore the other side of the basement, so I took a left down the hallway. Maybe there would be another exit. But when I entered the large dark cavern, I saw omegas sitting on the cold concrete floor and conversing with each other. There were three of them, and they were dressed poorly in rags with dark bags under their eyes. They looked dejected as they sat on the floor, looking at me curiously.

"What you in here for?" asked one of them, nodding her chin towards me. This omega had a nose piercing and purple-dyed hair. She looked like she was the youngest of the group.

"I don't want to talk about it," I said, not sure how much to trust these omegas. But I made it a rule to myself that I wouldn't trust anyone here except for Sergio, Ian, and Evan.

Walking around the massive basement, I saw a flimsy table with a slow cooker on it. I opened it, and a foul-smelling chili wafted in the air. I quickly closed it, and my nose turned up in disgust. Instead, I grabbed a piece of dry bread next to the slow cooker.

"That's the only food we got," said the purple-haired omega. "Every day, all day. So you better eat for strength."

"Are you serious?" I said, grabbing a tin cup and pouring water in it using a spigot that barely had water. The water was cloudy. This place was so freaking gross I wanted to get out of here as soon as possible. "How long have you ladies been here?"

"Don't remember," said the purple-haired one. "Could be months or years, who the fuck knows?"

"At least it's not years like Sylvia, who died here," said the blond one, shaking her head.

"I'm Olivia," I said, sitting with my thighs closed as tight as possible since Brett had ruined my leggings.

"Reyna," said the purple-haired omega, rubbing her pale face. She looked like she hadn't seen sunlight in years. "Make yourself comfortable because you ain't leaving anytime soon."

"I've been here a month," said another omega who had brown skin and long braids down her back. She pressed a hand to her belly. "I'm Monique, and they took my baby after I nursed him for two days."

"I'm so sorry, Monique," I said, hearing the sorrow in her voice. I couldn't imagine that happening to me. "Why did they put you in here?"

"Because I didn't willingly hand them my baby," Monique said, eyes downcast. "I fought for my baby boy until the end. They figured I wasn't loyal enough and didn't belong, so they dumped me in here as punishment."

"Once you're in here, you'll never get out," said Reyna darkly, leaning back on her elbows, and I could see marks all over her legs from living here. Her knees looked bruised, and I wondered what the hell happened to these omegas.

I looked over at the third omega. She had short blond hair, not much of it anyway since it looked like it was chopped off at the roots.

"I'm Krissy," she said in a timid voice, biting her filthy nails. It made me sad to see such a young omega in such dire condition like this. Dread was pouring through every vein in my body at the type of life they lived, and I got a glimpse of my future life.

"Why are you in here, Krissy?"

"I tried running away with Reyna," said Krissy, shrugging. "It seemed like a good idea at the time, but now I'm willing to do whatever it takes to leave. I miss the sun and being outside walking on the sand."

"I'm sure you do," I said, tears springing to my eyes as I chewed on the hard bread.

"I'm fucking sorry, and you know it, Krissy," grumbled Reyna, shutting her eyes tight and re-opening them.

"I know," sighed Krissy. "You never forced me to go with you. I went willingly."

"It doesn't matter. None of us should even be in here. The alphas are to blame," I said, the cold ground underneath me hard on my ankles. "Why don't you sit in the rooms instead? They have cushions, at least."

"During the day, we like to hang out here," said Monique, looking up at the tiny window high above us. "We'd rather not sit in the torture rooms all day long. We need a break from the memories the rooms hold."

My stomach twisted with fear.

"What happens?"

"The alphas," said Monique. "They come in here and knot us. Multiple alphas who haven't been assigned omegas but need to relieve their hunger come in here for the rebel omegas to take."

"What the fuck?" I asked, horrified, standing up. I couldn't be in this place locked up. I didn't belong here. "We need to get out here."

Reyna let out a sharp laugh.

"She thinks we haven't tried any of that before," she said, and that made my brain whirl in utter confusion. I looked up at the window and didn't see a way I could scale up the tall concrete wall.

I paced around the dark cavern, holding the dry bread in my hand until it crumbled to pieces on the ground.

"Great, you're going to bring in the rats now with that mess," said Reyna.

"Sorry," I said, my mind unfocused. Alpha after alpha would come in at night and knot us. The thought of it made me sink against the wall in horror. Rats were the least of my problems right now. "Brett brought me in here as my alpha handler. Would other alphas be in my room?"

"Yes, there are no locks in the rooms," said Monique. "It's a free-for-all basically. They don't care about us."

"What happens if you get pregnant?"

"You give birth upstairs and come right back in here. If any omega upstairs are unhappy with their baby taken away, they know they'll end up in here," explained Krissy. "They tell all the rules before omegas give birth."

"I couldn't allow them to take my baby," said Monique, breathing hard. It was like the memory was still fresh in her mind's eye. She looked distraught, and I felt the hopelessness emanating from her. "If only they could give me my baby back, I wouldn't care what they did to me."

Without any way to escape, I rejoined their circle and listened to their horrible tales of capture while thinking of my current horrors with Brett that were going to happen and which would only get worse.

In here, the omegas were treated like shit. No rules, no nothing.

And that thought alone scared me like no other.

Fourteen

IAN

"Where's she? I haven't seen Olivia all fuckin' morning," grumbled Evan as he dug into the bowl of oatmeal before him on the table.

I sighed, unable to talk about it for a moment. I had to reign in the rage I felt towards the asshole Henry. I had no idea why they took her, and without knowing what it was, I wasn't going to implicate Sergio.

"I know where she is," I said, staring at the empty plate before me. I couldn't eat all morning, debating what to do.

"Okay? Why aren't you saying it fast enough? I miss her."

"They took her to the Birthing Building," I said, crossing my hands behind my head, still unable to believe it myself. They didn't usually take omegas there for no reason, and I contemplated what could possibly warrant her being here.

"What for? She's not pregnant. Right?" said Evan.

"Of course, she's not pregnant," I said, knowing that Evan was slower to process information. "I don't know what the reason is, but apparently, she pissed off Henry enough that he decided she needed correction."

"Oh fuck," said Evan. "We need to tell Serg right away."

"I know," I said. "I wish I admitted that it was us who gave her the pills."

"But if that wasn't the issue, we would have been in trouble for no fucking reason," said Evan. "You did right by keeping your mouth shut. You need to tell Serg."

"Fine," I said, pulling my phone out. I didn't want to worry him needlessly, but this counted as an emergency. I wondered what they were doing to her now, and I wished I could bust her out of there immediately.

I sent Sergio a quick text but got a reply immediately.

> Yo, they took Liv

Where?

> To the birth building

Why? Did she go into heat?

> They wouldn't tell me. I tried to stop them.

She's in danger. U haven't seen half the shit I had over there. I need you to go there tonight, no matter what, and check on her. Break her out if you have to.

> That's impossible

I'm with the Royal Pack now.

> When are u coming back?

I fucked up. I can't come back until I have reinforcement with me.

> What did u fuckin do??

Can't say over text. Take care of Liv, please

I'll try my best

I sighed, pocketing my phone. Evan had read the texts over my shoulder, so I didn't need to explain what Sergio said. We looked at each other. Breaking into the other building without any reason or clearance was going to get us killed.

"What if we get caught?" said Evan.

"Then we died trying," I said.

"I want to save her and all, but is there any other way?" asked Evan, who had never broken the rules. He was also the one who never put heat suppressant pills for omegas either and insisted I or Sergio do it. "Need to be smarter about it, that's all."

"We're going there tonight," I said. "Get your gear ready and anything you need."

He nodded grimly, and I tried to think of the best way we could break into the building undetected. Because once we lost Henry's trust, it was all over for us.

But Olivia needed us. She desperately needed us at this moment to protect her.

Fifteen

OLIVIA

Tonight was going to be my first night here, and I was afraid to death.

Sitting on the dirty cushion with my knees pulled up, I stared at the closed door, losing all track of time. I had no idea if it was nine p.m. or midnight. Or if it was morning even. The omegas said they needed to sleep and rest up before the alphas came down here, so I sat here instead.

I didn't want to be caught off-guard by sleeping. That was my worst fear, which was worse than my fear of the dark.

The door opened, and I looked up from the cushion where I was drawing lines in the fabric with my finger. Upon seeing Brett at the door with his crazy eyes, I gulped in fear when I saw that he was holding a chain and a hammer in his hand. He barged into the room and slammed the door shut.

He stared at me, sniffing the air in deeply. Smelling my scent of fear.

"I missed you Button," he said. Then, noticing my look of fear at what he was holding in his hands, he laughed. "Don't worry. This is to lock the door before anyone else gets in here and takes you from me. You're all mine until you're pregnant with *my* baby."

Then he turned around to hammer in the chain on the wall and the door, chatting away while he worked. I didn't say a word as I listened to his madness. I was hoping his project of setting up the lock would take more time, but he finished it up way too quickly for my liking.

My heart started to beat faster again when he dropped his tools.

And his pants.

I couldn't look at him, and I didn't want to. I turned my face the other way when he climbed onto the cushion with me, kissing my shoulder. While he kissed my breasts and licked my nipples, I started to hear the screams outside my door.

The screams of the other omegas and the charging of alpha footsteps down the basement stairs.

I froze in fear while Brett sucked and kissed my nipples. Hearing their screams reminded me of the horror that awaited me. Being a virgin made it ten times worse since I didn't know what to expect.

"Lay down omega. On your back," he commanded, and I stiffly laid on my back as he licked my center. Over and over, he licked until I started to tremble, responding to his touch. As I stared at the ceiling, I heard knocking at my door, and all feelings of arousal disappeared within me.

"Please stop," I begged, trying to move away from his face.

"What did I tell you about telling me to stop? Didn't I tell you I would knot you right away if that happened?"

I breathed faster in fear.

"No, I'm sorry," I said, but he gave me a wide smile, licking his lips and gripping his penis.

"An alpha honors his promise, doesn't he? Like Henry said."

The voices outside my door sounded louder as a horde of alphas trying to break in. "You have to share, man!"

"Fuck you," shouted Brett while pushing himself inside me. I screamed as I felt the sharp pain of losing my virginity. I shut my eyes tight, tears in my eyes, wishing this wasn't real.

This was just a nightmare. A fucking nightmare, that's all.

But I couldn't block out the sounds of his grunts, the screams of the omegas, and the sound of the door breaking. With my eyes still closed, I felt the other alphas touching my body, heavy breaths on my neck. I tried not to breathe in their stench as they leered around me.

"Get off her!" shouted Ian's voice, and my eyes snapped open.

"Too late, I'm knotted inside her," grunted Brett, who was sweating and lying on top of me. I looked at Ian and Evan, who were flinging punches at the rest of the alphas in the room. I didn't even know how many there were.

I tried to wiggle away from Brett, but his penis had enlarged within me, trapping me to him. Chills went down my body in a panic.

This wasn't real. It couldn't be real.

It hurts.

But it was real.

"You're going to prison, Ian," said one of the alpha guards who jumped into the fray, dragging Ian off of another alpha and placing handcuffs on him. They did the same to Evan and marched them both from the room. Ian gave me one last despairing look, and I couldn't even muster a smile. I focused on them instead of the painful knotting that was happening inside me.

I was alone again with Brett. In the nightmare I was in.

"Those alphas aren't happy your boyfriends beat them up," Brett said while kissing my neck. "They'll be back to knot you next."

"It's not my fault," I whimpered, looking away from him but with tears streaming down my face.

"Now they think you're a valuable omega," said Brett.

"When is your knot going to release me?" I gritted out, trying to push his sweaty chest away from mine. I never thought my first knot would be an act of force and not love.

"A while," said Brett. "Don't you like it?"

"No," I said, my pussy painfully stretched around him. But the fullness within me from the knot felt like something I never felt before. It was foreign and strange but not unpleasant the longer it stayed inside me.

But I needed to block him out again.

"It's because it's your first time," said Brett. "The next time it happens, it will be more pleasurable. Your instinct is to be knotted repeatedly for the alphas. We own your body."

I was done talking to him as I looked off to the side, trying to block him out. I thought about my old life and how I wished I could go back to the mundane, boringness of it. I missed my family and friends more desperately at this moment than any other. Ian and Evan had come to save me, but now I lost all hope with that. They were taken, and now I had no one who knew where I was.

When Brett's knot released me, he got up without a word and put on his pants.

"You look nice dripping for me," he said with a smirk, and I quickly slammed my legs together.

He wouldn't get the privilege of staring at me after taking me against my will. He left the room, and I looked at the broken door, which I couldn't close for privacy anymore.

I could still hear the omegas out there gasping, yelling, or crying while the alphas ravaged them. I quickly sat up before the other alphas knew Brett was done with me, and I ran to the darkest corner of my room, huddling with my knees pulled to my chest in the hopes that they wouldn't see me.

I took long, deep breaths to calm my shallow, panicked breathing. But I couldn't calm down no matter what.

I felt violated and used. Worthless even.

Not realizing that my tears were flowing freely down, I cried as I sat on the concrete floor. I cried silently in the corner for long minutes until it felt like hours. I imagined my mother hugging me, telling me it was going to be alright. Her soft voice in my ear and my dads surrounding me, protecting me from everything.

"You are the glue who made our pack stronger," my mom, *Jade, once said to me during my birthday. "I'll never forget the day you were born on the yacht while I celebrated with your fathers."*

"How come, Mom?"

"The moment you were born was the best day of my entire life," she said, smiling. *"You are everything to me, and if anything happened to you..."*

"Don't say that, Mom. Nothing will happen."

She smiled sadly like she knew omegas were doomed from the beginning. "Let's pray nothing will happen. You are right, my baby."

I sobbed even harder, trying to wipe my tears away at the memory. My family felt like a ball of light in the darkness I felt in here. And only the memories of them would help me keep my sanity.

THE NEXT DAY, I didn't realize I had fallen asleep in the corner of the room.

My neck ached as I lifted my head off the cold floor, and my body was stiff with cold. My legs felt like noodles as I slowly stood up and walked to the cushion after not hearing any more screams outside. *It must be morning,* I thought.

I lay in the middle of the cushion, ignoring the wet stain underneath my thigh. I was too cold and tired to think straight. The ache between my legs hurt as I remembered Brett's evil look after finishing with me like I was nothing. His look of utter contempt upon seeing me cry.

He didn't give a fuck about me at all, and I never felt so low.

I heard light footsteps come into the room, and I opened my eyes halfway, seeing Krissy sitting at the edge of my cushion.

"Come and eat breakfast with us," she said. I shook my head silently, wiping my nose with the edge of my shirt. I didn't feel like going to the shared bathroom out there yet or eating the moldy food. "Staying holed up in here all day is not going to help, trust me."

"I just need to process everything," I said, my voice thick from crying and from sleep. "I feel like a piece of trash right now."

"That's exactly how I feel every night," said Krissy. "But you can't let them take your soul. They took your body but not your soul, Olivia."

I thought about that for a moment. But I also couldn't bring myself to muster up the strength to move.

"Maybe I just need more sleep."

"I always felt like sleeping forever was the answer. I never want to wake up the next day," she said. "But this is your new reality.'"

"Are you serious?"

It had finally hit me that I was here. And that I was here to stay as the permanent playmate for the alphas until the day I died.

"I'm serious, Olivia. And the only way you can survive is if you can take care of your soul even if they take your body as theirs," said Krissy, holding out her hand. "Now come eat with us, okay? This will be the best part of your day. Talking with everyone about other things will help."

And with that, I followed her out of my room to start my new life that I never asked for.

Sixteen

SERGIO

"You're back," said the commanding officer of the Royal Pack.

He sounded bored as I sat on the other side of his desk in his office. I was the complete opposite of bored, ready to tell him more information regarding the omega breeding camp.

"As you know, Henry is still breeding omegas," I said. "I have pictures from the Birthing Building."

Reaching inside my jacket, I pulled out the polaroid pictures of mothers in sterile white rooms and a large circular room where they kept the babies.

"Do you have proof that the omegas have been brought there by force?"

"Jareth, you know they have," I said, exasperated and annoyed. He was scratching his mustache and looking at me like I was stupid. "I was sent on a mission myself to kidnap a young omega."

His eyebrows rose, and I remembered the recording I kept of Henry telling me to do the job.

"Is that so?"

His question made the hairs on the back of my neck rise.

He gave off the same vibe that Claws had, and I decided to hold back from showing him the recording. I would have to find the king and talk to him directly. He didn't look interested, and something seemed off this time.

"Yes," I said, staring at the dusty family portrait on his desk.

Something about the picture caught my eye, and it wasn't the three kids sitting at their father's feet. It was the father himself. He looked nearly identical to Henry but older. Then, my eyes roamed to the kids, and I focused on one of them. Something about his features looked familiar. He had black hair and looked like the younger version of Henry. My pulse raced when I saw the second kid next to him, and it looked much like the commanding officer in front of me.

What the fuck?

"What are you looking at?" Jareth barked.

"Are you related to Henry?" I asked in bewilderment, not intimidated by his uniform or muscular physique. Jareth contemplated my question, sizing me up before he answered.

"It's not a secret that he's my brother," said Jareth. "I suggest you leave my office right now."

I stood up from the chair, giving him a calculated look.

"I don't know what your problem is today, Jareth, but we really need to help those omegas," I said. "We need to go in there today."

"We're not ready," he said, pursing his lips.

"Don't you want justice for them?"

"Of course I do," said Jareth. "But we don't have the resources yet to take on such a huge operation. I will take it under consideration."

"I see," I said, and then I turned to leave, even more determined to find King Armon myself.

Luckily, I didn't have to wait long before I bumped into

him in the gardens, talking to his omega wife and drinking tea. After the guards had escorted me out, I was able to lie and pretend I had more information. But instead of going to the commanding officer's room, I turned in the opposite direction.

"Sergio," roared King Armon upon seeing me walking towards him and his wife.

"My king," I said, bowing. And I kissed the queen's outstretched hand. "My queen."

"Do you have news from the breeding camp? I haven't heard anything in years."

"Years?" I asked, arching my eyebrows. I knew Jareth was up to no good. He was protecting his damn brother. "Sir, I have a lot to tell you."

After I finished relaying everything I had been telling Jareth and everything my pack had informed him about, the king's face turned white.

"Such horrible news," said his wife. "What are we going to do, Armon? Those omegas need us!"

Suddenly, I heard footsteps crunching behind me, and I turned, seeing a gun pointed straight at me.

"Did you fucking tell him?" growled Jareth.

"Fuck," I muttered, hoping he wouldn't lose it. But I was willing to die for the omegas trapped in there. I was willing to die for my mother, who had disappeared in there years ago.

"Put the gun down," said King Armon calmly. "Or else we will kill your brother on sight. I know you don't want that."

At the mention of his brother, Jareth slowly lowered his gun.

"You won't kill him?" asked Jareth.

"We will bring him in for questioning," said King Armon, nodding to his guards, who instantly pulled the gun away from Jareth, putting handcuffs on him. "Take him to the prison for treason. I will deal with him later."

"You'll regret this," hissed Jareth, his black eyes narrowed into slits as they took him away.

"Thanks for that," I said to the king, and he nodded gruffly. He wasn't happy at all how things turned out. Especially finding out that his commanding officer was corrupt couldn't be easy.

"I will send my best force with you to the camp," promised King Armon. "We will take Henry down and put an end to this nonsense. Alphas have gone astray plenty of times, including myself, but I cannot allow this to go on. It was all a rumor before, but now you've confirmed all the atrocities. I appreciate all the effort you've put in, Sergio, but we'll take it from here."

~

Three Days Later

IT HAD BEEN days since stepping foot back onto the OBC grounds.

But this time, I had reinforcement.

An army of alphas silently jumped out of helicopters and cars, surrounding the two buildings in the middle of the night. I couldn't believe I had managed to convince the Royal Pack that this operation needed to end after finally getting through to King Armon.

Holding a rifle in my hands, I ran as quickly across the sand.

I needed to get to my pack first and find out where Olivia was. I hadn't been able to contact Ian for days after telling him to check on Olivia, and I was worried something horrible had happened to him and Evan.

I shot at the two alphas guarding the entrance to the lobby, and they collapsed to the ground, unsuspecting of me.

Their blood seeped into the sand, staining the ground below.

Barging into Henry's office, I could see his feet on the desk as he smiled at something on his phone. His eyes bugged out of his head when he saw the massive rifle in my hands.

"Greetings," I said curtly. "Where's Ian and Evan? My pack."

Henry slowly removed his feet off the table. And he must have pressed something under his desk because I could hear alarms blaring throughout the building. Long, loud ringing blaring through my skull.

"They're not here," he said, interlocking his fingers on the desk. "I suggest you leave right now before I order your immediate execution. You don't want to die before you save your precious Olivia, do you?"

"Where are they?" I said, cocking my gun. I had enough of his nonsense, and I was ready to shoot the fucker down now. But a voice at the doorway distracted me.

"They're at the barracks, in the prison cells," said Rodmon, who was pointing a gun at Henry. "Can't believe the Royal Pack guards are here."

"They're here?!" roared Henry. "You did this, Sergio. Do you find satisfaction in destroying everything I worked so hard for?"

Every fiber in my being roared at me to pull the trigger. To put an end to him.

"I'll watch him until he gets arrested," said Rodmon, gruffly shaking my shoulder. "Go. Go get your pack and your omega."

I didn't need any more pushing.

I rushed out of his office and outside towards a smaller building behind this one. The sand flew under my thick black boots as I held the gun over my shoulder. I wished I could shift into my alpha wolf form to get there faster and to get Olivia quicker, but I needed to be armed. Every second mattered, and every second, she was probably getting tortured.

I hoped she was okay, and I prayed furiously in my mind as I got to the barracks. There were no prison guards as they were rushing to help Henry, ignoring me in the mix, thinking I was still loyal.

I stopped one of the prison guards running towards the building.

"I need the keys. Henry said he needs all the backup that he can use," I barked.

The guard threw the ring of keys at me without a second look at my face.

"Serg is here! Thank god," said Ian, grabbing the iron bars and shaking them to the other prisoners' annoyance.

"Oh, thank fuck," said Evan, who stood up from the dingy ground, joining Ian.

"It's not like he has the keys or anything," said one of the other prisoners.

"I do," I said, shaking the keys, and suddenly all the prisoners surrounded the door, ready to rush out. They were all in here for disobedience to Henry. "I'm breaking out all of you to help the omegas free."

"You got it, man," said one of the larger alphas covered in tattoos. "The love of my life is trapped in there. And she just had a baby a month ago."

When I shoved the iron gate open, every alpha shifted to wolf form, howling as they escaped out of the giant cell.

"Where's Olivia?" I asked.

"We'll take you there," said Evan quickly, shifting into wolf form as well as Ian. They ran ahead of me towards the tall glass building that no alpha without clearance was allowed into. A place where all the babies were born and sent to foster care for no reason.

Gripping my rifle with now-sweaty hands, we made our way to the building despite the chaos of alphas shouting and omegas screaming. I had to get to Olivia, despite the short time I'd known her.

I shot the lock on the door, and we burst into the building.

Ian and Evan bounded down the steps of the basement in wolf form. It got darker and more rank the further down I climbed. The stench down here was unbearable, and my eyes widened upon seeing three skeletal-like omegas sitting together in the main cavern. They looked almost shocked to see us there.

"But it's not time yet," said the one with the long braids, with a shocked look on her face.

I looked around, not seeing my precious Olivia anywhere. "Where's Olivia?"

"In her room," she answered, and my pack ran there. The other two omegas looked frozen in place as if scared to draw my attention to them. I felt sorry as hell for these omegas, and I wished I had gotten here earlier.

"You are free to go," I said, pointing the gun up the stairs. "It's unlocked. The Royal Guards are out there, and they have cars to take you."

"You don't need to tell me twice," said the purple-haired omega, making a run for the stairs. When the other two omegas didn't see me shoot their friend, they made a dash for the stairs.

Catching my breath, I was nervous about the state of condition that Olivia was in.

I ran down the dimly lit hallway and saw a room with a door that was hanging by its hinges. Walking towards the room, I saw Ian and Evan parked at the doorway, refusing to go inside.

"What's going on guys?" I asked with dread. I was so fucking scared to find her dead inside. The thought shook me to the core, and when I heard Ian whine, I rushed into the room.

And when I saw her, my heart shattered.

She was hiding in the corner, covered in a shroud of darkness, with her face tucked between her knees. Putting the gun behind my shoulder with the strap, I slowly approached her so as to not scare her further. She was visibly shaking when she heard me approaching.

I stopped and knelt on my knees.

"Olivia, it's only me," I said in a low voice so she wouldn't get scared even further. I was worried she would go into shock from the tremors in her body.

"No, no, it's not real," she muttered to herself, shaking her head.

I inched closer, my heart breaking even more when I saw her filthy leggings or what was left of it. Her feet were stained from the black paint on the ground, and her arms were covered in scars.

"It's very real, Liv," I said, and she slowly looked up. Her curly black hair was matted to her scalp, and her eyes were red, either from lack of sleep or crying. Her lips were trembling when she tried to speak, but she was overcome with emotion-her eyes flooding with tears.

"It's really you," she said, gasping for air, and I quickly made my way over to her. I lifted my arm to wrap her in a hug, but she flinched, and I stopped myself right away.

What kind of fucker would do this to her? What the hell happened to her?

"I'm here to take you home," I said softly. "Don't you want to see your family again?"

Her eyes widened.

"Yes," she breathed, trying to straighten her legs to stand, but she was shaking so much. I offered her my arm, and she hesitated before taking it. Her cherry scent enveloped me as she leaned on me for support.

We took two steps before she froze, her body tensing against mine. She stared at Ian and Evan at the doorway, who were both howling in victory.

"Oh, that's just Ian and Evan," I explained.

Her shoulders relaxed slightly. "Okay."

I desperately wanted to scoop her up in my arms and get the fuck out of there, but that would only make her retreat back into her corner. All the signs of mistreatment were there. I would question her once we were on the plane, as doing so now would do no good for us. She wouldn't trust me, and I needed her to. I helped her up the stairs while my pack ran ahead of us, still in wolf form.

Gunshots and chaos still reigned outside. I was glad to see omegas being taken into vans, planes, and cars as they evacuated the premises. I led my omega to the black private plane awaiting us, and her eyes widened when she saw it.

"Wait, we need to save the others," she said, turning back to the building, but I held her arm.

"They're all being rescued right now," I said. "The Royal Guards will make sure they're safe."

She nodded silently, a tear pouring down her cheek.

Seventeen

OLIVIA

With shaking legs, I climbed up the stairs and into the plane.

I had never been on a plane before, and the old version of me would've been excited. But the excitement was overshadowed by the misery I endured for three nights in a row. Everything felt like a dream as I walked inside with my filthy bare feet onto the pink plush carpeting. It was like a bed underneath my feet, and I felt some of my tension releasing.

I gasped when I saw how huge the plane was.

The entire lounge had white luxury chairs set in a circular pattern. As we walked towards it, we passed by individual private rooms with alpha-sized beds inside and vases filled with plants. The plane was filled with ambient lighting, which set a peaceful contrast to the night sky outside.

"Is it okay if I use the bathroom?" I asked the short flight attendant who was leading us to the lounge.

"Of course," he said, straightening his blue vest. "Alphas, the lounge is to your right. I will escort this young lady to the bathroom."

"We'll be waiting for you right here," said Sergio and I nodded. His eyes held compassion and pity that I couldn't face yet.

I couldn't talk to him about any of it at all.

"Okay," I said, following the flight attendant further down the plane, and he opened the door with a flourish. It was a huge bathroom with enough space to fit ten people. There was a golden toilet, a huge tub in the middle, and a shower as well. "It's huge."

"It is," he said proudly. "Enjoy, madam."

I walked into the bathroom and locked the door behind me. The heated floors under my feet felt nice as I sat on the toilet. Everything still felt like a dream to me, and it felt like I was walking around on clouds. I still couldn't believe I made it out of the OBC when it felt like I was never going to escape. But now that I was free, it felt like I was missing a part of my soul. It felt like my soul was torn in pieces, and I had no idea how to patch myself back up again.

After I finished using the toilet, I stood for a while, staring at the shower and standing outside the glass door. I felt so unclean after my time at the camp that it looked so appealing to me right now.

Peeling off my dirt-encrusted clothes, I stepped into the shower and closed the glass door. *Were guests even allowed to use the shower?*

I had to wash off every touch and every liquid that Brett had left on me. When the warm water hit my cold skin, I sighed with pleasure. The shower was everything I dreamt of. My stomach muscles squeezed painfully while I stood there under the water.

I was probably just hungry after days of being stuck at the camp, so I ignored the tight squeezing of my abdomen, which happened again when I grabbed the shampoo bottle. Lathering the shampoo in my hair, it felt so good doing normal tasks like this again. I massaged the shampoo into my scalp, feeling my tension decrease from being in fight or flight mode for days.

But when I closed my eyes, all I could see was Brett's smirking face when he thrust into me one last time, and my stomach squeezed painfully again.

Breathing hard in a panic, I opened my eyes and quickly squeezed out the shampoo. I couldn't let my mind go there. If I thought about everything that happened, I would surely lose my freaking mind.

Then I heard knocking on the door.

"Ma'am, we're about to take off," I heard the flight attendant say, and I hurriedly turned off the water after rinsing off.

I had never been on a plane before, and I had no idea that I wasn't supposed to be in here until after we were in the air. Drying myself off with one of the neatly folded towels, I searched for something to wear in the mini-closet they had.

I had to wear either my soiled ripped clothing or a silk bathrobe covered in floral design. Picking the latter, I threw it on and tied the rope really tight so it wouldn't fly open since I wore nothing underneath. I wish they had underwear, but I guess they assumed that the traveler would have their own outfits.

I had nothing on me at all. I had no money and no clothes.

The bathrobe flowed to my ankles, and my hair hung in wet curls around my shoulders. I rolled up my filthy clothes in a ball and stuffed it into the trash with satisfaction. Before leaving the bathroom, I grabbed a miniature bottle of lotion, and I was happy that the cramping in my belly had at least stopped for now.

When I joined the alphas in the lounge, they all looked up at me when I walked in hesitantly. I forgot how to act normal around them.

They weren't out to get me.

I sank into one of the cushioned chairs between Ian and Sergio. The soft feel and fabric made it feel like I was sitting on clouds. It was amazing as I looked out the window.

The plane started to move, and I was nearly jolted off my chair. I instantly grabbed Ian's hand during takeoff, and he squeezed my hand comfortingly until we were finally in the sky.

"Sorry," I said bashfully. "I've never flown on a plane before."

"It's okay, sweetheart," said Ian in the gentlest voice. "You can hold onto me whenever you need to or whenever you get scared. I don't mind, Livvy."

"Livvy?" I asked, my lips quirking into a smile.

"I can call you just Liv if you don't like it," he said.

"I love it," I said, my heart pounding as we locked eyes, but I quickly looked away towards the window. It was so beautiful and peaceful, gazing at the night sky as slow music played in the background over the soft hum of the engine. The cabin was dimmed with little periwinkle lights on the ceiling, and the table between us was covered with little bowls of snacks.

I don't think I'll ever get used to this type of luxury after my experience.

"Look, they're trying to escape," said Evan, pointing at something in the distance outside. I squinted in the darkness of the cabin, making out a speedboat in the ocean and Henry running around it. There were even omegas on the boat that he was trying to take with him.

Loud shots rang in the air, but the speedboat continued moving. My mouth was open in shock as I watched it all from high up in the air. Everyone on the boat ducked down, waiting for the next shot. I turned away from the window, feeling ill and breathless. I only cared if the omegas were okay.

To hell with the alphas.

A flare of the pain I felt earlier hit me again in the belly.

"What's wrong?" Sergio asked me in concern, his hand on my arm.

"I think I'm just hungry," I said, and he immediately started barking orders to the flight attendants to get me food. "It's not an emergency."

"It is," he said gruffly. "I'm sure they starved you in that dingy place that they forced you to sleep in. I'm so sorry you had to endure all of that crap. When you're ready, you can tell me everything that happened to you. But for now, I want you to eat and get some rest. Okay, Liv?"

Relieved that I didn't need to explain myself to anyone, I nodded.

"Thank you, Sergio," I said.

When my steaming hot plate of pasta with vegetables arrived, the smell of it instantly hit my senses. Taking bite after bite, I couldn't slow down until I felt another flaring pain in my belly that made me pause.

"She must be hungry," said Ian while Evan agreed with him.

"Are you excited to see your family again?" Evan asked me. "I'm going to miss you."

"Unless she wants to be our omega," muttered Ian.

I bit my lip, unsure how to respond to it. "I'm more than excited to see my family again. But I'm not ready to be an omega for *any* alpha pack. I feel so broken after what they did to me."

"Of course," said Sergio. "Don't pay attention to them, Liv."

I continued to eat until I finished every bite of food from my plate. I settled it carefully on the table and laid a hand on my stomach. I needed time alone right now, and I wasn't ready for normal, civil conversation.

"I'm going to get some rest in the bedroom," I said.

After closing the door, I gasped with pain, holding my

stomach and dragging myself to the bed. The excuse of hunger was no longer there, and I began to freak out about what was happening to me. I curled up on the bed over the comforter since it was too painful to move, and I closed my eyes. Everything still felt like a dream, and maybe I'd wake up in the nasty dungeon room with the three omegas I'd made friends.

Through my pain, I wondered where they were and if they were able to escape. Hopefully, they were able to escape like I did. The pain passed again, and I slowly drifted off to sleep.

"Suck harder, useless omega," screamed Brett when I faltered around his cock. Then he shoved himself down my throat until I gagged. But I forced myself to hold back the bile and finish. I didn't want him there any longer than needed, so I would take care of him fast.

Pitch black room and screaming sounds from tortured omegas.

I needed to hurry, and I tightened my lips around him until he came. Hot liquid dribbled down my chin, forcing me to swallow his seed that I didn't want.

"Good girl," said Brett, patting me on the cheek. "Now lay on your back, and let me taste you again. Aren't you a good omega?"

Eighteen

SERGIO

"I'm fucking glad you were able to get through to the Royal Pack the way you did," said Evan.

"I know," I said, chewing on a biscuit and reclining my chair. "They were the ones who sent me here in the first place."

"True," said Ian. "Sooner or later, they'd have had to put an end to the operation. Do you think Olivia will agree to be our omega?"

"She needs time, Ian," I sighed. "She had gone through unspeakable hell. And I have every intention of finding out what happened to her and hunting down whoever hurt her."

"The night we were arrested," started Ian, and I sat up straighter in my chair. "Brett was in the middle of full-on knotting the poor girl."

"Wished we could have ripped his fucking dick off," said Evan. "Before they dragged us away."

My breaths came out shallower, and my throat tightened.

"Did you say Brett? The blue-haired fucker?!" I asked, trying to keep my voice low but couldn't.

"Yes," Ian confirmed, and my head spun.

"He should have been killed before we got on this plane," I gritted out, not realizing I had squished the biscuit into smithereens. "When we land, that will be our mission. To get revenge for our omega. We will kill the bastard no matter what it takes."

"Yes, sir," said Evan, his chest puffing with righteous anger.

I couldn't believe Brett was that fucking evil. He wasn't a friend or enemy of mine and mainly just lurked about.

He was a nobody to me.

Until tonight.

Just then, I heard Olivia cry out, and I immediately got off my chair, dropping all the crumbs onto the carpet. I rushed to the room and saw her beautiful form tossing and turning on top of the plush red comforter. Her left leg was exposed from her thin silk robe, and she was clutching her belly. Her eyes were closed, and tears were streaming down her face.

"Olivia," I said gently, tapping her on the shoulder. She was deep in her sleep, writhing in pain. I'd never seen her so scared. "Olivia."

She opened her eyes, and she was breathing rapidly like a caged animal. Staring at me with glazed, fearful eyes.

"Get away," she muttered, her words incoherent.

"Baby, it's me," I said, my heart shattering at the fear in her eyes. I never wanted an omega to be afraid of me like this. Especially not her. "It's Sergio, I would never hurt you."

It took her a minute to slowly out of whatever nightmare she was having.

"What are you doing here?" she asked, her eyes widening.

"You were crying in your sleep," I said, and she roughly wiped away her tears.

"Sorry," she said.

"Don't be. It's okay," I said, sad that the spunky Olivia was no longer there. Maybe one day she would return. But lately, it looked like she had lost her spirit and had become meek. Especially after what Brett did to her.

"Can...can you hold me while I sleep?" she asked in a small voice.

My chest swelled with pride. She was trusting me to hold her.

"Yes, baby, of course," I said, settling in behind her on the bed. She leaned her back against me as I wrapped my arm around her waist. She pulled my arm up to her chest, hugging my arm tight around her. "Do you feel a little bit better now?"

"Much better," she sighed softly.

"I won't let anyone hurt you, Liv," I promised her. "Never again will anyone hurt you. I will find Brett and hunt him down until he's dead."

She didn't reply.

Instead, I heard her quiet snores as she drifted off into sleep again. Her scent enveloped me as I hugged her. I didn't mind laying with her in bed. I loved cuddling her at the OBC, and there was no way I was going to falter in my duties now. She needed me to protect her, and I was going to do it.

No one was going to hurt my little omega ever.

Olivia

THE BRIGHT SUN woke me up, and I squinted as I stirred awake. I immediately realized there was an arm draped around me, and I gasped, startling the alpha awake.

"Oh, whoops, I completely forgot," I said in embarrassment as Sergio stretched. I watched the little tendrils of his hair covering his forehead as he yawned. "Thanks for cuddling me last night."

"Hey, it's okay," he said. "Did you sleep well?"

"I did," I said, and a hint of a blush crept up my cheeks. I felt like kissing him on the face, but I was too scared of that, and it might encourage him to take me right here. Suddenly groaning in pain, I stayed like that, hunched over and holding my stomach.

"You're in heat," he said in a gruff voice. "No wonder you weren't feeling well last night."

"I can't be," I moaned, trying to move off the bed, but I couldn't even move an inch without horrible pain and squeezing of my belly. "We landed and everything. I have to see my family."

"Listen to me, Olivia," he said slowly.

I didn't want to listen to him because I knew what he'd say.

"My family is waiting for me," I said urgently, cutting him off. I groaned through the spasm in my belly and the slick feeling between my legs. It was a horrible type of pain that could only be relieved with a knot.

"If we take you to your family's house now, they will send you to the heat clinic," explained Sergio slowly. "Because it's too late for any heat suppressant pills."

Suddenly, Ian and Evan came into the room, seeing me hunched over in pain while Sergio rubbed my back.

"What's going on?" asked Evan, rushing over to me and kneeling on the ground before me. Ian sat on my other side and rubbed the top of my hand, clutching my belly.

"She's in heat," said Sergio. "Olivia, would you want a bunch of strangers at the heat clinic to help you? Or us?"

I gasped, drawing in breaths to try and ease my pain. It was impossible to answer his questions with a clear mind, but I knew like hell I would never let strangers touch me again.

"Fine!" I said. "Just help make the pain stop. It's getting worse every second we talk here."

"I will take you to our home until your heat passes," said

Sergio, scooping me up in his arms. I leaned my face into his chest, breathing in his alpha scent. His scent triggered another attack, and I whimpered as he jogged to the exit of the plane and down the steps.

All of a sudden, we were in a limo, and I only knew it from the motion of the car on the road.

"Tell him to go faster," said Ian.

I wondered if they were talking about the driver. I imagined a big bald guy driving the limo for some reason through the haze of my pain.

"You shouldn't have left me at the breeding camp," I said to Sergio in a low voice. I had no idea why I was telling him this right now. "They hurt me when you left."

"And that's why I'll never leave you again," growled Sergio, rubbing my back as he held me on his lap. "I will keep you safe, Liv. You know that, right?"

"I don't know," I muttered, my eyes rolling back at the intensity of the pain in my abdomen. "You're a nice alpha and all, but I've seen the dark side of alphas. They're all animals deep down."

"Not all," said Sergio. "I promise you that not all alphas are the same."

"Are you sure?"

"Yes."

"How come you were at the breeding camp? Why couldn't you get a normal job?" I asked. Suddenly, I screamed when my belly squeezed viciously. "I need a knot right now!"

"Hold on, baby, we're almost home," said Sergio, panic in his voice. Then to his men, "he needs to fucking hurry up and drive faster. She's getting worse."

"What if I don't get knotted at all?" I said, wondering what would happen. I would take my chances.

"You might go into shock and possibly die if you go too long without a knot."

God, this was horrible.

I couldn't fucking believe I was in heat right now, and Brett had accomplished his life's mission in ruining my fucking life. Now, I would need a knot, and I had no idea if I would be pregnant after it happened.

It was all fucked up, and it felt like my life had turned into a joke.

More slick gushed from my pussy, and I wondered if Sergio could feel me on his lap. No matter how tight I squeezed my thighs together, the slick was oncoming and rapid. The fear of getting knotted again was more than my fear of the heat. Brett made knotting as painful as possible for me. He didn't wait for me to get ready and would be knotted inside me by the time I opened my eyes in the darkness.

"We're here," said Sergio.

"Finally," I said. Then, in a lower voice. "Can you knot me in private? Like just us? I don't want everyone together in one room."

He looked confused by my request, but he nodded right away.

"Yes, whatever makes you comfortable, Liv."

"Thank you," I said as he carried me out of the limo and rushed to the house. I turned my head to see a huge brown home, and it looked rustic, like a cozy cabin. I loved the look of it, but the painful heat reminded me that I didn't have time to just admire stuff.

In seconds, Sergio carefully laid me on a bed.

"We will knot her one at a time," Sergio told Evan and Ian.

"What?" said Evan.

"Close the door and wait out there until it's your turn," commanded Sergio. "I will knot Olivia first and make sure she's okay. Then Ian is next, then Evan. Unless she has a different preference."

"It sounds...good," I moaned through the pain, my eyes shut closed as he gently separated my thighs.

"Look at me, Liv. I'm not taking you by force," said Sergio. "I want you to keep your eyes open and on me so you know it's me."

I gulped.

"Okay, but if I get scared, I'm closing my eyes again."

"If you get scared, I'll stop right away," said Sergio, and I looked at him with shock. An alpha never stopped during mid-rut. He kissed my knees while holding my gaze, and I bit my lip in uncertainty.

He wasn't being forceful with me, and my muscles slowly relaxed, allowing him to spread my knees apart, and my silk robe fell open.

Nineteen

SERGIO

She was frightened. I could tell by the way she glanced between my face and the ceiling.

The corrupt alphas had done a number on her, and my heart raged for her. I wished I didn't have to do this now until she was ready, but she was in heat. She had to be knotted immediately. I couldn't help but drink in her intoxicating scent as I kissed her knees and her thighs. Every inch of her seeped the ever-sweet cherry scent that I loved. Olivia was like no other omega I had ever met.

"Please, Serg, I need your knot," she said.

"I will give you my knot, baby," I said. "I need you to open your legs for me wider." She complied, and I gazed at her dripping pussy lubricated with her natural omega slick. I pressed my finger gently into her, and she immediately clenched around my finger.

"You have to let me in, sweetie," I said. "I'm not here to hurt you. I'm only here to help you, and because I love you."

Her eyes widened.

"What?"

"You heard me, Liv," I said. "I realized while I was gone

that I missed you. You are the omega who holds my heart and not because I'm about to rut you. It's because we're fated to be together in this moment."

"Oh," she said breathlessly while spread open before me. Her pink delectable pussy ripe for a knotting. "Can we talk more about this after you knot me?"

"Of course," I said, gripping my hard dick. I hastily removed my pants, eager to be inside her warm tightness that was waiting for me. I couldn't let my rut take over, and I could already feel the alpha instincts within me fighting to emerge.

To rut his omega. Over and over until she was with child.

Gritting my teeth to fight my insane urge to rut her senseless, I gently pushed myself into her, watching her flinch in response.

"You okay?" I asked her, stopping myself from entering her completely. Her warm tight pussy lips clung around the tip of my penis, and my heart thundered in my ears from how horny I was. I hadn't realized the impact of how it would feel to enter an omega after years of abstinence. "Look at me, sweetie."

She took in little gasps of air and nodded.

"I'm okay," she said. "Please keep going. I'm in so much pain, but I'm not going to break. Just please knot me."

I pushed further inside her without constraint this time. I allowed myself to sink in deep, enjoying her hot little pussy clenching around my dick. She wrapped her legs around my waist as I thrust in and out of her.

Every thrust pushed my cock deeper inside her. She wrapped her fingers around my arm as she watched me enjoy her pussy.

Fuck.

Her long, dark eyelashes fluttered as her mouth opened in desire and arousal. Her face was flushed, and her breasts jiggled under her silk robes. Pushing aside her robes, I exposed her breasts and grasped one of them as I thrust harder.

I was close.

My cock began to heat up as I thrust faster and faster. Harder and harder until she moaned, tightening her legs around me.

"You feel so fucking good," I said. I roared as I exploded, her legs widening for my knot and her pussy clenching harder around me. "I'm going to knot you, sweetheart."

I felt my racing heartbeat start to slow as my cock enlarged at the base. Every pump of my semen going inside her made my chest swell with joy at knotting my omega.

My omega.

She was mine even though she wasn't sure yet about me.

"Oh, that's instant relief," she said, her head relaxing back against the pillow as she kissed my arm with her soft, warm lips. "Thank you so much."

"Don't thank me," I said, kissing her on the lips, and she smiled with an uncertain look in her eyes. "I know you don't want to get attached or anything, but I'm trying my best not to give you a mating mark right now."

She was breathing hard as if she wanted it too, but the slight worry in her eyebrows stopped me from doing exactly that. If I bit her and marked her, she would belong to my pack. For me and my men. And it was proving much harder to hold back than ever before.

But I couldn't lose control.

"I brought food," said Ian, coming into the room and placing a plate of spaghetti on the bed.

"I could definitely eat right now," she said, licking her lips with her cute pink tongue. I adjusted her so she was sitting on my lap while we were knotted together, and I took the fork from Ian, trying to feed her. "I can feed myself."

"Let me take care of you, little omega," I said, and she

blushed. Her pink cheeks reddened even more as she took a bite from the fork. To me, it was the most intimate thing an alpha could do for his omega. "I had always dreamt of knotting and feeding my future omega."

"Mhm," she said, closing her eyes as she savored the taste and wiggled over my knot in contentment. "Is this your room?"

The room was heavy with our scents mingled together, and the bed sheets mussed all around us, creating a nest I hadn't intended. My room was the largest in this house, with wall-to-wall curtains over the large windows and a flat-screen television.

"It is," I said. "Do you like it?"

"I like how roomy it is," she said. "But it's a little depressing and dreary."

Ian laughed, and I glared at him.

"Why aren't you out there with Evan?"

Ian immediately looked over at Olivia in a panic. "I'm sorry, I forgot. I'll hang outside until you're done."

"It's okay," she said gently. "I...I'm okay now. I was just a little scared at first. Since you know..."

"I know," breathed Ian in relief. "You look so beautiful knotted and getting fed by Serg."

"Oh, stop," she said, laughing gently. "I don't have a choice with this heat. It feels horrible being an omega right now."

"Don't say that, sweetie," I said, feeding her another bite and enjoying the way her sensuous lips closed over the fork. "You make the perfect omega. We will help you through your heat so you don't feel a single pang again."

Evan soon joined us in the room, and I stayed knotted inside her. After I was done feeding Liv, I leaned against the headboard and caressed her arms lovingly while she laid her head on my chest. Ian was rubbing her back, and Evan was massaging her feet. She was content and comfortable for now, which was all I wanted.

"What are you thinking about?" she asked me, looking up with those large lashes of hers.

"Just happy that you're here and that you allowed me the honor of knotting you," I said. "How about you?"

"I'm excited to see my family again," she said. "I can't believe the nightmare of the camp is finally over. It just doesn't feel real sometimes."

"Do you live with your family?"

"I do," she said. "Can I borrow your phone to let them know I'm okay?"

"Ian, grab me the phone," I said, and he paused massaging her shoulders to grab my phone off the nightstand.

He handed it to her, and we tried not to listen in as she talked to her mother. I could hear her mother crying on the other end of the line and her soft reassurance that everything was okay now.

Slight disappointment settled within me when I heard how excited she was to go home, and my cock twitched inside of her, already mourning the loss of our beautiful omega. *Fuck, I needed to get a grip.* If she didn't want us, that was her choice and something I've been fighting for since the beginning.

And if she wanted me, I was never going to refuse her.

Twenty

OLIVIA

"You're so beautiful when I knot you," said Sergio as he stroked my hair gently while I was knotted to him on the bed. The relief from his knot felt amazing and not painful at all. I tried not to think about the dark room at the OBC, but it was hard not to sometimes.

"I'm glad you think I look pretty," I said, smiling bashfully. I felt like a hot mess, sweaty, and my hair crazy ever since my heat began. His cock was slowly sliding out from me, releasing me for the next alpha.

Evan was cleaning up and taking away my empty plate of food while Ian spooned me from behind. Sergio's eyes roamed to my lips, and my heart started to beat faster, longing for him to kiss me.

"May I?" he asked, and I nodded slowly. I closed my eyes as he lowered his face to mine, kissing me gently despite the longing I felt from him. "You taste...so sweet."

I blushed, and my pussy started to clench again with the lack of a knot inside me.

"I need a knot again," I said, embarrassed to death. "I thought my relief would last longer than a couple minutes."

"Ian will knot you next," said Sergio. "I understand that you're confused by this. Is it your first time going into heat?"

"Yes," I said. "I didn't realize how crippling this entire thing is."

"I know, sweetheart," said Sergio. "It's why I try to help out omegas back at the OBC and prevent their heats from coming."

At the mention of the camp, a dark, gloomy mood settled over me despite my clenched pussy walls.

"Take a deep breath, Liv," said Ian from behind me. His hand was wrapped around my waist. "I could feel your breathing pattern changing. Don't panic. You're with us now and completely safe."

I breathed in deep, and the panic started to dissipate.

"I will step out of the room so you can have some privacy," said Sergio, and I didn't protest as he left the room, shutting the door behind him. Maybe being cuddled between two alphas was too much for me right now.

"He's probably right," I said as I turned to face Ian. "It's easier for me when it's one alpha at a time."

"You don't mind if I hunt down the alphas who did this to you and kill them, right?"

I giggled, "I won't mind at all."

"Then it's a promise, baby," said Ian, kissing my forehead. "Now...why don't you feel how hard my cock is for you?"

Trailing my hand down his chest speckled in blond hair, I watched his chest rise and fall faster with his breathing. His erect cock waved up and down before I reached it. I took my time rubbing his naval area to arouse him even more. I enjoyed this game of making him wait in anticipation until he let out a low rumble of impatience.

"Why are you so mad?" I teased, finally wrapping my fingers around his hard member, and he let out a groan of pleasure. "Oh, you're so big. I'm a little worried how it'll fit inside me."

He seemed to grow another two inches in my hand as he pushed himself into my hand. I squeezed tighter, rubbing up and down. Then he reached between my legs, rubbing my already drenched pussy covered in slick mixed Sergio's semen.

"Your pussy is so beautiful and warm," he said, sliding a finger inside of me. "Cute as a button."

My brain started to whirl, and I released his cock immediately.

"C'mere Button," said Brett smirking at me. "Crawl to me and take my cock into your pretty little mouth. Now, will you do that for me?"

I was shaking and crying, overwhelmed by the sudden memory.

"Open your eyes, Liv," said Ian.

"What's going on?" barked Sergio, rushing into the room with Evan as I opened my eyes. I lay there on my back, limp and shaking after the horrible flashback. "What did you do to her, Ian?"

"He didn't do anything," I gasped. "Just please...don't say that word around me. Please, just for now."

"What?" said Ian, looking lost as released my vagina. "What word? Tell me, and I'll never say it around you again, baby."

"It's silly," I said, breathing hard and trying to come down from my panic as my pussy clenched painfully over and over. "Try not to say the word 'button' around me. I know it's stupid, but he used that name on me. I just try to block it out, and every time I do, the memories come back stronger and more terrible."

"That fucker will die for this," growled Sergio while Evan agreed, cracking his knuckles.

"Fuck, I'm so sorry," said Ian, looking remorseful. "I swear you'll never hear it from my lips again."

"It's okay," I said, sitting up and leaning against the headboard of the bed. Sweat was running down my forehead from the warmth of our nest and my sudden panic. My breathing was still rushed, and my limbs were trembling.

"Focus on something," said Sergio, sitting before me on the bed. Sitting cross-legged but not touching me. "Focus on something and hold your gaze there."

"Okay," I said, looking up and deciding to look into his eyes. His kind brown eyes calmed me enough to slow my breathing. His eyes were beautiful and held a depth, an alphahood that I grew lost in.

"We're not here to hurt you, Liv," he said slowly. "And it's hurting me to see you in pain. Just breathe."

He very gently laid a hand on my outstretched leg, and I placed my hand over his. I focused on his eyes and only his eyes until I started to feel myself calming down.

"I feel a little better already," I said, my breathing starting to even out and slow down. "How did you know what to do?"

"I grew up in a foster home and around other kids who had panic attacks all the time," he said. "I watched how my foster mother calmed them down."

"I'm sorry you had to grow up in a foster home," I said.

"Thankfully, my parents who adopted me were good to me," he said. After talking with Sergio, my mind was in a different place, and it was impossible to think about Brett while Sergio talked about his life.

But the pain from my heat was getting worse, and the stabbing pains in my belly increased rapidly. My pussy walls clenched repeatedly, reminding me that I needed a knot, and it grew worse as we talked.

"The pain is getting worse," I suddenly gasped.

"Are you ready to try again?" asked Ian, and I nodded,

laying back down as he gently spread my legs apart. My pussy throbbed as I watched him, Sergio, and Evan all gazing at my pussy.

"I'm ready," I gasped, swallowing as another stabbing pain rushed down my belly. "Please, Ian."

"Look into my eyes while I take you," he commanded, and I looked up, meeting his blue eyes. "You're with me safe and sound."

Then he pushed his hard cock into me, stretching me and stopping my pussy from clenching so painfully.

We gazed into each other's eyes as he thrust into me.

Gazing into his eyes felt different, taking me to a different level of intimacy. This didn't feel like rutting but more like love-making, which caused my pussy to throb with need.

"Oh, this is so good," I moaned as Ian kissed me on the mouth.

"Do you want me to play with your clit?" asked Evan, and I nodded frantically. I felt Evan's finger swirling around my clit as Sergio watched carefully. I looked at Sergio, and I could see his hard penis between his legs as he gazed at me with an orange glow in his eyes.

It turned me on even more, with Sergio watching Ian fuck me on the bed like this.

"Am I making you nervous?" asked Sergio. "I can leave."

"No, stay," I said, breathing hard as Evan rubbed my clit harder in circles and Ian's cock pulsed between my legs. I turned back to Ian and gazed into his eyes. The butterfly feeling in my belly increased, and my pussy clenched tight around him.

"Fuck," growled Ian, pushing deep into me.

Hot liquid streamed inside me, and I screamed with ecstasy as Evan rubbed my pulsing clit.

"Good girl," said Evan, watching me twitch and gasp underneath Ian. He released my clit, and Ian leaned down to kiss me on the mouth again while his cock swelled inside of me.

The knotting brought me instant relief from my heat again.

His cock swelled and stretched me wide, holding my walls apart.

"You did it, baby," said Ian, his lips on mine as his long blond hair covered us both. "You're so fucking brave going through your heat like this."

"Thank you," I said, smiling against his lips. "Your knot feels so amazing inside me. It's just so magical."

"My magical knot," chuckled Ian. "I like it."

"I'm going to buy us dinner," said Sergio, kissing me on the cheek. "Are you okay here, sweetheart?"

"Yes," I said, looking back at him. His gaze was the most intense and caused me to blush every time.

"Evan will take care of you next, and we'll have a nice dinner together," said Sergio. "What type of food would you like me to get?"

"Anything," I said. "How about a juicy steak?"

"It'll be here," he promised. "Now, let the alphas take care of you. Do you trust me, Olivia?"

"I do," I said. "I just can't control when my memories happen."

"When it happens, let us know," said Sergio and I nodded. "Look into our eyes, and you'll know you're not in that wretched place."

When he got up and left the room, I snuggled closer to Ian while Evan hugged me from behind. It felt good to be cuddled between the alphas that I trusted. A warm fuzzy feeling started to arise within me as I gazed at Ian's chest while he lazily played with my thigh.

"My knot inside you feels so fucking good," he said, and I smiled. "I don't want this to end."

"Me too," I said. "I was just thinking that."

"Because it brings you relief, or because you like me?" he teased, but I could tell he was half-serious.

"Both," I said without missing a beat. "I have feelings for all of you, even before I went into heat. It started when you both held me in your arms while dancing."

"Not even during our first kiss?" asked Ian.

"Not as much as how I felt after," I said. "The more I get to know you guys, the more I start to have feelings for you."

"Mhm," said Evan, kissing my neck, and I smiled. "I think I'm in love already."

Twenty-One

OLIVIA

"I wonder where Evan went," I said twenty minutes later while knotted to Ian. Ian's knot was slowly starting to release me, but Evan had disappeared for that entire time.

"He's probably cleaning his room or cleaning some part of the house," said Ian, holding me closer to him. "Can't I just knot you forever to me?"

"Thank god that's not a thing," I said, giggling. "How would I get anything done?"

"We would just hire servants," said Ian while his cock released me.

"I would feel guilty making them work so hard," I said, brushing his hair back. He had a rogue look about him that made him look like a rebel. Like he couldn't care less as he broke the rules. "Were you a bad boy growing up?"

"Hush," he said, kissing me. "Now, where's Evan? Because if he doesn't get back here in five minutes, I'll just knot you again."

"Ooh, someone's greedy," I said breathlessly against his lips, and his tongue pushed into my mouth, claiming me. I loved being around Ian, and I briefly wondered how it would feel to be theirs forever. Some part of me longed to belong to a pack, and another part of me was scared.

"I have a surprise for you," said Evan's gruff voice from the side of the bed.

Startled, I pulled away from Ian. I didn't even hear him enter the bedroom.

"Eek! I didn't hear you," I exclaimed.

"Ian was busy hogging you all to himself," growled Evan, lifting me in his arms and I squealed.

"Careful there, buddy," said Ian.

"You okay, babe?" Evan asked me, looking deep into my face with those slanted green eyes. His handsome looks never failed to take my breath away.

"Yes, I'm not a piece of glass," I said, and he chuckled.

He carried me out of the room and down the brightly lit hallway. The house was huge, and I couldn't wait to get a proper tour of it when my heat passed. But after my heat, I would see my parents, and it would be amazing. I couldn't wait to see my mother's smiling face and my dads' look of relief on their faces.

"Right here," said Evan, setting me down on my feet in the bathroom. In front of me was a steaming hot bath with bubbles and red rose petals floating on the top. His thoughtfulness made my heart beat faster.

"I can't believe you did this for me," I said as he slid my soiled silk robes down my shoulders, and I let it drop to the ground. I couldn't wait to get into the tub. The water warmed my legs as I stepped into the tub, careful not to splash all over the pristine bathroom.

"I would do anything for you," said Evan, getting into the tub and sitting next to me. He placed his arm around my waist and squeezed my hip. "Do you like it?"

"I love it," I moaned, leaning back and allowing the water

to ease my cramps. It felt so fucking good to be in here after a couple of knottings. "You're a romantic alpha."

"I watched a lot of movies," he said, grinning with a crooked smile. It made his handsome face even hotter as I stared at him. He licked his lips. "Why don't you sit on my lap, babe?"

My heart raced as I straddled him face-forward while his cock sat underneath my pussy. Our privates were touching, but his cock wasn't penetrating me yet, so my heart was beating a mile a minute. The soapy water swirled around my breasts, and he lifted some of the soap, rubbing it around my left breast.

"What are you doing?" I asked.

"Playing with you," he said, squeezing and releasing my breast under the water. "You have such full tits, and they feel so heavy in my hand."

I touched his shoulders, dripping water all over his neck with my soaked fingers. Swishing the soap around in the tub, I relaxed as he weighed my breasts in his hands, and I massaged his neck with my soapy hands.

It was relaxing for me. No pressure, and the heat of the tub eased my cramping a little.

"I'm going to need a knot soon," I sighed, resting my chin on his right shoulder. "I just want to relax and have fun."

"I know, babe," said Evan. "How about if I stick my dick inside you right here?"

"I don't mind," I said, wanting to play more with him, but my pussy and womb were insistent that I needed a knot at this very moment. His strong hands lifted me by the waist, his cock slowly spearing into my pussy.

Every inch of him entering me felt delicious.

My slick eased the passage inside of me so it didn't hurt. Hazy steam from the hot water surrounded us, and it felt like a dream as I gazed into his eyes through the steam.

"Fuck, you're so tight," he said, pressing his lips against mine. We kissed like that in the water with his penis straight up inside me. It felt good, and it felt right as our lips meshed over one another, causing me to become breathless. "I'm going to bounce you on my cock, babe. You can tell me to stop anytime."

"It's okay, I can take it," I said, eager for him to knot inside me and bring me the relief I craved as an omega. Squeezing my hips, he lifted me straight up and down onto his cock, assisting me as I rode him. I threw my head back and moaned how good it was. The feeling of his thick cock stretching me in the water nearly made my eyes roll back in pleasure.

"Do you like that baby?" he asked, bouncing me higher onto his cock. The water splashed over the rim of the tub, creating a mess on the floor as I bounced on him.

"It feels so good," I moaned, flexing my pussy, and he tightened his hold on my hips, not letting me escape or move. He was in full control now, and it turned me on as I turned off my dark thoughts. He lifted me up and down like a rag doll, stretching my pussy to the limit.

"Fuck!" he growled, shooting loads of his come inside me as he smashed me over his cock until he began knotting inside me. I squirmed on his cock, still horny but nicely filled, so I reached between our connected privates. "What are you doing, babe?"

"I just need a little bit..."

"Let me touch it for you," he growled, moving my hand aside, and I felt his thumb rubbing my clit.

"Oh yes, like that," I moaned as he flicked my clit back and forth, making me squirm on his cock that was now locked inside of me. Every flick of his thumb sent a zing of electricity shooting through my belly until I shattered around his pulsing dick.

He kissed me on my open mouth, drinking in my orgasm

as I moaned against his lips. I trembled in his arms as he held me tight in the water. He held me like that while we both took in what just happened while he knotted me.

He plopped soap onto my nose.

"Hey," I protested as he chuckled.

"You're so cute," he said, taking my hand as I swatted the soap from my face. "You look like a little reindeer."

With my other hand, I took a handful of bubbles and rubbed it all over his hair in vengeance. I laughed, seeing his look of bewilderment. I brushed his hair back with my fingers, touching his jawline and caressing his face.

"Why are you so freaking hot?" I muttered, and he grinned at me.

"Can't help it, babe," he said. "You're way too good for me."

"No, I'm not," I said.

"I can't imagine being with any other omega, ever," he grunted, kissing my shoulder. It was so magical and quiet in the bathtub, with the sounds of the water plopping onto the ground and our hushed whispers.

I wanted it to last forever. But I couldn't.

"I wish I could be your omega," I said, swallowing away my nervousness. "But I need time to process everything that happened."

"I know, no pressure," said Evan. "I'm just letting you know that there's an opening available for you to be my fated omega girlfriend."

I giggled, and he hugged me close to him in the water.

"Your idea of a tub is the best," I said. "I feel so relaxed, pain-free, and clean at the same time."

"I thought you'd appreciate it," he said. "I never helped an omega through a heat before, and I always imagined it to be in a crowded nest filled with sweaty males and semen flying everywhere."

I laughed and slapped him lightly on the arm.

"Don't be gross, Evan," I said.

"You know it's true."

"I guess, but once you're in a rut, it's hard to think of stuff like that," I said. "I've seen alphas in rut, and it's not pretty."

He rubbed my back as I laid my head against his chest.

"I wished I did more when I saw Brett do that to you," said Evan. "Wished I could have killed him. But Sergio will make sure that happens."

"What if he comes back for me?" I said, starting to get nervous about the possibility of Brett finding me.

"Most likely, he's been taken to prison," he said while purring into my neck. *How the hell did alphas talk and purr at the same time?* His chest vibrated against my resting head, sending chemicals of calmness through my body.

"But what if he isn't in prison?"

"I'll never allow him to get near you if that's what you're asking," said Evan. "You have us to protect you if you choose to be with us forever. Forever, you'd be safe until the day you die."

"Oh," I said, shocked by the intensity of his declaration and passion. He was actually serious that he'd fight for me. "You are all amazing to me, and I feel safer around you. Without a doubt, but like I said, being an omega for a pack scares me a little."

"Don't stress," he said, kissing me again on the lips. "Whatever you decide at the end, I'll respect your decision. We would never mark and take an omega by force."

I nodded gratefully, and for the next few minutes, we relaxed, hugging each other in the water for the duration of him knotted inside of me.

Twenty-Two

OLIVIA

After my bath with Evan, I walked into the bedroom and saw Sergio placing several shopping bags on the bed.

"What's in those?" I asked curiously, clutching the towel around my chest.

"I'm going to get dressed in my room, babe," said Evan, kissing me on the lips. The water dripping down his tanned skin was a sight to see.

"Okay," I said, and he left the room, winking back at me when he caught me checking out his muscled ass cheeks. I smiled and shook my head as I turned back to Sergio, seeing him laying out lotions and perfumes on the dresser.

"I went and bought a few stuff that omegas usually want," he said. "Stuff that you might need."

"Why thank you," I said. "Thanks for thinking about that. Not many alphas are that thoughtful."

"You were exposed to the very worst of us," he growled, carefully placing the brand-new combs and hair sprays next to the perfume. "I also got you some underwear and clothes you might need. Wouldn't want you to sit naked at the dinner table tonight, but actually, on second thought..."

"Don't even," I said, walking over to where he was arranging everything. I dropped the towel onto the plush carpet, used to everyone seeing me naked by now. But I could hear him stop what he was doing. As I squirted lotion onto my hand, I could see him from the side of my eye. He was pretending to organize the toiletry, but his head was turned towards me.

"What are you doing?" he breathed.

"Just putting on the lotion you bought for me," I said. "I mean, you've seen me naked before."

"Ah...yes, that's right," he said, sitting on the edge of the bed.

"Are you just going to sit there and watch me?" I asked, amused.

"Just to make sure nothing happens to you," he said. "We can't leave you alone during your heat. It's the most crucial time for an omega."

Turning around, my back facing him, I rubbed the lotion around my arms. Even though I just had Evan's knot, I was already aching between my legs again for the next knot.

My omega body was intent on getting pregnant. *Oh my god. How could I have been so stupid?*

The panic around my heat made me completely forget about getting impregnated by this pack.

"Sergio," I said, turning around with lotion all over my hands.

"Yes?"

"We can't do this anymore," I said. "I never planned on getting pregnant. What if I get pregnant?!"

"It's why I bought condoms as well," he said, pulling out a green box from one of the bags. "Hopefully, you didn't get pregnant so quickly, but an omega's heat is unpredictable, and this was an emergency situation."

"But what if I get pregnant?"

Panic streamed through me at the thought. I wasn't ready to raise a child alone. I wasn't successful like my cousin Lacy, and I didn't have a stable job.

"I'll take care of you, I promise," said Sergio, licking his lips. "Even if you decide you don't want me as your alpha, I will make sure to take care of you. Now don't you worry, alright, my love?"

"Fine, I won't worry about it," I said, continuing to slather on lotion on my legs. But in my heart, I was definitely worrying. *What would my family think of me? What would I do with a tiny baby?*

As I bent down, lost in thought, I heard Sergio's heavy breathing behind me.

"Stay just like that," said Sergio, and immediate excitement pulsed through me. My heart pounded hard as I stayed bent over and held my ankles for balance. I could see him approaching me, and I suddenly felt something cold press against my pussy. "I want to see how you look like all plugged up."

I swallowed as he rubbed the cold glass around my pussy.

"What are you doing with that?" I breathed.

"I'm going to put it in your ass. You would like that, wouldn't you Liv?" he asked, setting my skin ablaze as he grasped my ass cheeks apart. My breathing was erratic now, and I was getting even more horny at the thought of him staring at my hole.

"I can try," I said. Before getting kidnapped to the OBC, I had experimented with putting things in my ass to stretch myself out for my future alpha pack, but I'd been too scared to push a toy in all the way.

"Stay still, little omega," he said, swirling the lubricated toy around my asshole. I could feel the rounded end seeking entrance into my butt, and I bit my lip in anticipation. My heart was pounding so hard I thought I might collapse. He slowly inserted the toy, and I gasped. "Don't clench sweetheart. Let me in."

I took a deep breath and felt him push the plug inside further.

Stretching my ass.

"Oh, that feels weird," I said, feeling the toy rub around my anal walls as he pushed it in further.

"Touch your clit," he commanded, and I reached between my legs shyly. "I can see how wet your pussy is for me. You're very excited."

I felt slick dripping down my thighs at his words, and I couldn't help but obey him. I rubbed my clit with one finger while he swirled the toy around my anus. Around and around until the toy stretched me even more. I rubbed my clit faster, and he started to pump my ass with the plug. He pulled it out but not all the way, and then he would plunge it back in, making me see stars.

Moaning, I pressed my clit even harder.

"Do you like watching me rub myself?" I asked him, all my inhibition gone from how aroused I was. All my shyness disappeared in this moment. I just wanted to be his good little omega right now and be taken by this pack leader.

"I absolutely love watching you," he said. Then I suddenly felt something big press against my pussy hole. "And I'm going to knot you right here if you don't mind."

"I don't mind," I said breathlessly.

I could feel his thick cock pushing into my pussy and the rubber of the condom he had on. I rubbed my clit faster as he stretched my pussy with his cock and my anus with the plug. He shoved the toy all the way into my ass, and I cried out in pleasure, feeling the hilt of it hit my sensitive sphincter.

"I want you to lean against the edge of the bed," he said, and I turned to the bed. I laid my head against the pillow as he bent me over the bed. "Fuck. You look so pretty plugged up and with my cock inside you at the same time."

"Thank you," I moaned as he pushed his cock deeper inside me. I gripped the sheets, feeling the fullness in my ass bounce inside of me as he thrust into my pussy.

His balls slapped against my thighs with every thrust of his huge cock inside my pussy. He gripped my shoulders, pushing me down further onto the bed as he grunted behind me. Each sound of his grunt had my pussy throbbing and clenching repeatedly around his cock.

"Your pussy needs to be knotted before dinner," he said, shoving himself even deeper until I cried out. "You're such a good omega, aren't you?"

"Yes," I said, my face heating up with his praise.

"Why don't you clench your pussy one more time for Daddy Alpha?" he said, and I suddenly orgasmed around his dick. I was trembling as the powerful orgasm burst through me, and I could hear my pussy squelching with slick.

Each thrust made the squelching grow louder while I shook from the orgasm.

"Daddy Alpha," I gasped, collapsing on the bed. He continued to thrust into my pussy from behind and pushed the anal plug into my ass to hold me still.

"Fuck yes!" he roared as he pushed into me one last time. He exploded inside of me, gently thrusting until his cock swelled and connected us.

He was breathing hard above me, his hot breath on my neck as he tried to catch his breath.

I felt proud in a way. This was way different and pleasurable than what I had in the dark room. I was able to experience extreme pleasure in knotting with this alpha pack, and I didn't want it to end now.

"Oh my goodness," I said. "I didn't see that coming."

He lifted me until we were lying in bed with him spooning me from behind with his dick knotted inside my pussy.

"Just had to test out the condom," he said innocently. "Sorry if I was a little rough earlier. It's really hard to control myself around you, but I'll try to do better next time, sweetheart."

"It's okay," I said. "To be honest, I enjoyed every minute."

"That's good to know," he said, kissing me on the back of my head. "I thought I scared you, and that's the last thing I want to do."

"I think the more time that passes by, the better it'll be for me," I said. "It seemed like it was just yesterday that I was freed."

"It *was*," he said. "I don't expect you to feel normal after what you went through. If you wanted, you can experience a whole new life with a pack of alphas who care for you and take you to remarkable places for vacations."

"And restaurants?"

"Yes, and restaurants," he laughed, and I blushed. I had only been on a couple of cheap dates with alphas back in college. Nothing spectacular or romantic. We'd just grab a pizza or go to the movies.

"Well, that's good to know," I sighed in pleasure, wiggling myself over his snug knot.

"Will you wear the plug in your ass during dinner?" he asked, and my eyes widened. I was glad he couldn't see my expression.

"Umm, why?"

"To stretch you out," he said. "To teach your butt before we knot inside it."

"I don't think that's happening," I said, terrified at the thought of a full alpha's knot inside my ass. "Sounds pretty painful."

"You'll enjoy it," he said, kissing my neck. "Just promise you'll wear the plug tonight."

"Fine," I said. "But no knotting inside my ass."

"You got it, honey," he said.

"Dinner's ready!" shouted Ian from downstairs.

"Took his sweet time, didn't he?" said Sergio.

"Oh no, I need to take another shower before dinner," I groaned. "I'm so sick of this heat making me horny all the time."

Sergio chuckled, "Sometimes you say the oddest things, and it's just so cute."

I pressed my back even closer to his chest and smiled as he wrapped his arm tight around me. I closed my eyes, feeling his knot pulse inside my pussy and the feeling of his hot white liquid streaming inside me.

Twenty-Three

OLIVIA

Alone in the bed, I laid on my back for a few moments after Sergio left the room. I needed to get ready for dinner. But I wondered how the hell I ended up in an alpha pack house. And in their bed.

I knew their feelings were real. I could just feel it.

Getting up from the bed naked, except for the toy stuffed between my ass. I reached behind me to feel the type of toy he plugged into my ass. The end of it felt like a like glass ball, and when I wiggled it around, bolts of arousal zoomed through my butt area.

Oh whoa.

I never felt like this before in my ass, and maybe it was true that I could possibly slick from my anus. I experimentally walked around the room with the toy in my ass, and each step was a turn-on. The plug was heavy in my ass, stimulating every nerve as I walked. Reaching my hand back there, I twirled the plug around and around until I started to moan.

Oh god. I needed to stop.

I had to eat food before I made my heat pain worse.

The cramps took longer in between knottings now, which

was a nice relief for me, so I needed to eat. Releasing the anal plug, I walked to the bathroom and washed up first after Sergio's knot.

Then I dug around the shopping bags for something to wear. I found a nice red lingerie set with a lace red robe matching it, and I put that on, feeling sexy in it. I fluffed my hair and put on red lipstick that I also found in the bag.

Sergio had thought of everything.

When I was ready, I took a moment, taking in a deep breath, and touched my warm face as I looked in the mirror. The girl looking back at me was so different than when I used to live at home with my parents.

My eyes looked worn and tired like I aged before my time.

I wondered if I would ever go back to the innocence I had back in the past, thinking that all alphas were meant to protect and love their omega.

But I knew that wasn't the case. Not ever again.

As I walked down the stairs, I heard the men conversing in the kitchen, their voices excited. Maybe they were all relieved to get out of the treacherous camp, or maybe it was just I who was the happiest about leaving since alphas didn't need to suffer like omegas.

"Oh wow," I said, seeing the huge spread of food they'd prepared for me. They hadn't started eating yet, and Evan pulled a chair out for me across from Sergio, who was at the head of the table. Sergio's eyes were on me as I surveyed the meats and side dishes. "The food looks delicious."

It was quiet except for the clink of dishes as we passed around the mashed potatoes, macaroni, and different varieties of meats. My stomach was growling when I finally dug in. The alphas' chewing was loud as they also dug into their food viciously like alpha werewolves would do in the wild if they caught a deer. My heat had definitely affected us all.

"How's the pain?" asked Ian, touching my arm gently.

"It's okay, but I could feel it coming back," I said, biting my lip. "I don't want to be a bother or anything. I'm sure I could hold off with the pain for a little bit so you can all rest for the night."

"Nonsense," said Sergio with force in his voice. "My men and I will keep you satisfied for the duration of your stay. You will feel no pain while you have us. After dinner, Ian will knot you next, and we'll rotate from there."

Oh damn.

"I guess alphas don't sleep during an omega's heat," I said quizzically.

"It is what it is," said Ian. "I'd rather have an omega than not have one at all. And if I was to have an omega, it'd be you."

"Aw, you're sweet," I said, blushing as I ate the next bite. "I'm lucky to have you guys help me through this until I get home."

"Sure you want to go home after your heat?" asked Evan, winking at me. "We'd really miss your company."

"Yes, I'm sure," I said a little more sternly, just in case they got any ideas to keep me here. But I knew in my heart they wouldn't do that.

As I cut into a stubborn chunk of glistening smoky meat on my plate, I started to feel my pussy clenching again out of nowhere.

My belly started to contract, and I couldn't ignore it anymore. I groaned in pain, dropping my fork and knife with a clatter.

"Sergio, no," said Ian, and I looked up to see Sergio getting up from his chair. His eyes were glowing yellow as he gazed at me with a feral look. He started sniffing the air, and when my slick seeped from me, he darted around the table towards me. "Sergio!"

I didn't know what was happening, except that Sergio's

eyes were glowing weirdly and that he wasn't saying anything as he rushed towards me. He started sniffing my neck, inhaling my scent like a drug. Panic began to settle in me.

His eyes reminded me of something. Something dangerous and feral.

An alpha in rut.

My breathing started to escalate as panic rose within me. I got up from my chair and backed away from him as he stalked me to the kitchen.

"Sergio, please calm down," I said, holding my hands up as tears poured down my cheeks.

He blinked, and his eyes widened as he looked at me.

"Serg!" shouted Ian, holding him back with his arms interlaced over his chest. Evan ran into the kitchen to help out.

But at that moment, Sergio roared and shifted into werewolf form right there in the kitchen as I screamed. Then he suddenly bounded out the front door, howling into the night.

Gasping and shuddering, I leaned back against the kitchen counter with a hand over my chest.

"I'm so sorry," said Ian, breathing hard as he also looked out into the night, listening to Sergio's howls. "He nearly lost it there, overcome with his rut. Your smell is intoxicating."

"He needs to have better control over himself regardless of her smell," said Evan, hugging me. I laid my head against his chest. I was scared half to death, thinking he would rut me by force.

I felt Evan's chest rumbling and realized he was purring to calm me.

"Does that happen to you guys, too? Like the rut taking over?"

"What?" asked Evan.

"The rut thing," I said, breathing hard. My inner omega wolf craved for Sergio to take me like that, but after what I'd been through, it was a lot to take in. I couldn't handle something like that right away, even if contraction-like bands squeezed my belly in mortal pain.

"No."

"I have good control over it," sighed Ian, closing the front door without locking it. "When a rut takes over an alpha, the only thing he could see in front of him is the omega in heat. Whatever she wants is his to fulfill. And if she needs a baby right away, he can smell it in her scent."

I could feel Evan's dick pressing against my stomach, and my pussy throbbed in response as Ian spoke.

"Oh," I said. "I think I understand it better now. They need to teach more of this in schools."

"If they do, then the alphas would lose control at the mention of an omega in heat," said Ian, looking down. I followed his gaze and caught sight of his hard cock pressing against his pants.

My tears had dried, and all I could think about was getting knotted again. So I gripped Evan's penis over his pants.

"I'm an omega in heat," I sighed, nuzzling my nose against his chest. "And it sucks, and it's wonderful at the same time."

"Let's get you back into the bed, shall we?" said Evan, lifting me in his arms as I squealed.

"*I* was supposed to knot her next," said Ian and Evan smirked. My gaze turned dreamy as I stared at Evan's face. *Fuck, he was handsome as hell.* Every toned line on his face made me horny and made me forget what had just happened with their pack leader.

Sergio

THE SAND of the beach rushed underneath me as I sprinted in the dark in wolf form.

I nearly lost control. I scared her.

Raising my face to the moon, I let out a long howl of despair and stopped running. After I was sure I had calmed down enough, I shifted back. Now walking on two legs naked, I walked around the beach, shocked at myself.

I never lost control like that. Not ever.

Her scent sent me into rut mode almost immediately during dinner tonight, and she had called me her daddy alpha earlier. But remembering her red face, trembling hands, and tears made my rut dissipate instantly. I wanted to kill the alphas who did that to her. It horrified me that I made her so scared of me. Seeing my car parked on the road, I opened the unlocked door and sat inside for a bit.

Opening the glove compartment, I pulled out a wrinkled brown piece of paper that I had held onto for years. Tears glazed over my eyes at the disappointment I felt in not finding my mother at the OBC. I had joined for no fucking reason, and at least the only good thing was that we helped hundreds of omegas not go into heat right away. The whole thing had started out with me discovering the letter in my foster mother's room. I knew I was adopted, but I had no idea where I had come from until I confronted my foster parents.

I smoothed out the sheet of paper over my steering wheel, reading her beautiful handwriting one more time. As I read the letter, my eyes burned with tears that I couldn't control. I had failed my birth mother in finding her and protecting her. It had been years, but I at least hoped to get a clue on where she was. I read the letter one more time before putting it away:

To the future parents of my dear baby,

Please take good care of him as I cannot care for him at this moment. Even though I only held him for a few minutes, I know he is my baby, and he will return to me. But if you have an ounce of goodness in your heart, please care for him as if he were one of your own. Tell him that his mother will always love him no matter what.

Love,
Sylvia

Twenty-Four

OLIVIA

Evan gently set me down on the bed in the dark room, and I sat up, grabbing Evan's arm. I could feel the alphas' tension and anger arise in their need to take me first.

The rut was a powerful thing.

"You guys, I have an idea," I said, already very aroused at what I was going to suggest. The anal plug was driving my arousal up the wall, and the slick between my legs was nearly a flood by now. "I want you both. At the same time."

"Are you sure?" asked Ian, his voice breathless as he slid into the bed to my right, and Evan sat to my left. It was so dark in the room by now, but we didn't bother turning on the lights.

They immediately flipped me over, and I landed on Evan's chest, face forward. My heart raced with anticipation.

Ian grasped my butt cheeks, twisting the plug in my ass, and I gasped. I gripped Evan's cock in my hands while he fingered my pussy. I heard one of them throwing down a shopping bag from the bed, and I suddenly remembered.

"There's condoms in there!" I said, and Evan groaned. "Please."

He quickly snatched it up from the ground, and I heard the snap of the rubber as he reached between us to put it on. I gripped his cock again, which was now covered with the condom, and he slid his finger deep into my pussy.

"Your pussy is very wet and gushy for me," groaned Evan as I gripped his penis harder, rubbing it up and down in the dark. "Fuck, this is hot in the dark."

Ian continued to play with the toy in my ass, thrusting it in and out of me.

"I have to make sure you're stretched out enough to take my knot," said Ian, kissing my ass cheeks in turn. His warm lips pressed down onto my ass cheeks, turning me on so much as he plopped the toy out.

"I can't get enough," I said, grinding on Evan's finger, which was already deep inside my pussy. "I want your dick inside me."

"Alright, baby," said Evan, planting my pussy onto his cock. I moaned out loud at the exquisite feeling of his girth pushing inside of me and stretching my pussy apart. "I've teased you long enough, and now you'll get knotted as a reward."

"Please," I moaned against his lips as I rode him.

My naked breasts were smooshed against Evan's sweaty chest while Ian separated my ass cheeks apart, swirling his finger in the middle. It wasn't a shock since I had the toy inside my ass for hours.

"Your asshole is very cute," said Ian. "I like how it clenches around my finger."

I felt my pussy clenching around Evan's cock, and he groaned underneath me, gripping my hips with his hands in desperation.

"I want to fucking knot you," said Evan at the moment

when Ian's finger slid into my ass, and I bucked. Evan cradled my face and kissed me on the mouth as he lifted his hips up to meet mine, thrusting furiously.

My heart raced when I felt Ian trying to press into my ass with his cock as Evan bounced me up and down.

"I'm going inside you," muttered Ian, plunging his cock into my ass at the right time, and I gasped against Evan's mouth. My pussy and ass clenched around them both, greedy for their knots.

I was horny and ready for their knots to relieve my heat pains.

"Are you scared of him knotting your little tight ass?" asked Evan, getting even harder inside my pussy since the thought aroused him.

"A little bit," I said. "But I want it."

"She needs it," said Ian huskily. "Fuck, this is the greatest feeling."

He gripped my ass cheeks, separating them further as he thrust into my butt while kneeling on the bed. The smell of alphas and the dark coolness of the room almost had my brain spinning into dark memories, but I forced myself to focus on them.

Focus on Ian and Evan. I'm safe with them.

My lower belly started to clench, and I cried out as an orgasm hit me from Evan's cock, hitting my G-spot repeatedly.

"She came," grunted Evan, kissing me again on the lips. Then he bucked his hips upwards, as he also came at the same time. And I felt Ian's cock press hard into my ass again in his final thrust while he orgasmed simultaneously.

When both knots grew and settled inside my privates, I lay weak and trembling between the two men. It felt so good to be knotted in both my pussy and ass. It was an incredible feeling.

I was lying between Ian and Evan, cuddled between them as I yawned.

"When will Serg come back?" I asked.

"Who knows," said Ian. "He'll be back regardless. There's no way he'll ditch you."

"Are you sure?" I asked. "He seemed pretty angry with me."

"Trust me, he isn't angry at you, sweetheart."

"Okay," I said, closing my eyes. "I'm so tired."

"Get some sleep, little omega," said Evan, kissing my forehead as Ian kissed my shoulders. "Sleep while our knots are inside of you. It'll be the best sleep of your life."

Yawning again, I couldn't fret any more about Sergio since the impending sleep was taking over. My body was weak and aching from having sex all day.

"Goodnight, my alphas," I said, half-asleep. I was not sure of what I was saying now, but I'd probably regret it later. "Love you."

"We love you too, baby," whispered Ian, hugging me tight from behind as he spooned me, and I fell into a deep sleep.

BRIGHT AND EARLY THE next morning, I carefully crawled from the middle of their sleeping bodies so I could use the bathroom. It had been a peaceful night, and I only woke up once in excruciating pain, which Ian took care of while Evan snored next to me. I looked around for Sergio, and my heart sank when I didn't see him.

The ache between my legs was a reminder of all the knotting as I brushed my teeth and showered. Washing my hair felt good, and a little self-care time was all I needed right now. I massaged my scalp with an extra lather of shampoo, just thinking about how I got here. The past few weeks of my life had been a blur, and I couldn't wait to get back into a normal rhythm again.

After my shower and putting on a fresh pair of black panties with a matching bra- I threw on a thin dress that Sergio had bought. The dress stopped just at my thighs, showing off my legs. I looked back at the snoring alphas and smiled. Ian looked carefree and relaxed with one arm draped across the pillow as he lay on his stomach. Evan's black hair was all mussed up as he lay sprawled on the other end of the huge bed.

It was best to let them rest until I needed a knot again.

I felt fine right now, with only small twinges of pain. Maybe the first day of a heat was the worst, but now it wasn't so bad.

I tiptoed out of the room, showered and fresh as I walked down the stairs. It felt nice not to have slick constantly running down my thighs, my pussy eager for the next knot.

My pussy twitched at the thought.

Hmm...some tea would be nice, I thought. As I walked into the living room, I saw a bundle of bright orange roses sitting on the dining table with a note next to it. I looked around the room for Sergio and realized he still wasn't home. *Where the hell was he?*

Picking up the letter, I quickly zoomed through it and grew upset with every word:

Dear Liv,

I'm so sorry for what happened last night. I should have controlled myself around you more, and there is no excuse for what happened. It wasn't your fault at all, sweetheart. I'm going to stay away for your own safety until your heat's over, and Ian will take you home. It was the greatest pleasure to have known you. You are the strongest, most beautiful omega I've ever met.

Keep your chin up, honey, and don't hesitate to call me if you ever need anything. My number will be on the back of this letter.

With all the love,

Sergio

Sighing, I folded the letter and left it on the table as I went into the kitchen. I didn't want Sergio to just up and leave. I thought we'd at least talk about it, and something nagged at my heart to see him again. Maybe it was for the best that I didn't see him again so I wouldn't be saddled with a pack. But my heart was torn at the thought of never seeing him again.

I poured water into the teapot and watched it over the electric stove, waiting for it to boil while lost in my thoughts.

"Livvy," said Ian, joining me in the kitchen. "You look upset, baby. Was it the letter Sergio left for you?"

"You saw it?"

"Yeah, it was left on the table."

"Oh," I said, sighing.

"But are you okay?"

He wrapped his arms around me from behind, and I leaned into his chest for comfort. His wide chest was warm, and it felt right pressing up against him. He nuzzled my neck, waiting for an answer as he purred into me.

"I didn't want him to leave completely," I muttered as I stared at the tea kettle. "Do you have tea in this kitchen? I didn't look into the cabinets or anything."

"This is your home whenever you're here," he said.

"Not until you get a new omega," I said, the thought hurting my very being.

"That's never going to fucking happen," he said, nipping at my neck and I gasped.

"Did you just mark me?" I asked.

"I didn't draw blood, so no," said Ian. "Wish I could if you'd let me."

"Where's the tea, Ian?" I said, pulling away from him in a panic.

"I'll get it for you," said Ian. "Don't get mad at me, please. I just wanted to let you know how I felt."

I sighed. "It's just hard not to get attached when we're constantly having sex all the time, and now I already feel the pain coming again."

"I understand," he said, dropping a packet of tea into a mug as I watched. Then, he carefully poured the boiling water into it. "I've never helped an omega through a heat before, and I already think of you as mine."

"But I'm leaving after my heat ends."

"And you'll come back to us," said Ian confidently. "There's no way you're not feeling it, and you told me that you loved me last night."

"I...I did?"

Fuck. I was so tired from all the knotting that I was saying all sorts of things last night. Exposing my heart was the last thing I wanted to do since this wasn't a long-term type of thing.

"You sure did, my love."

Twenty-Five

OLIVIA

Three Days Later

"Oh yes, more," I moaned as Evan and Ian took me at the same time. I was sweating profusely as they both thrust into me while standing. I was skewered between them while they lifted me, pumping their cocks furiously.

It was our last day together after I spent a few days with them through my heat.

"This is us saying goodbye to you," Evan grunted heavily in my ear. He was deep inside my ass, his mouth pressed to my ear from behind.

"A nice sendoff for our pretty little omega," said Ian, who was inside my pussy. Over the past few days, he was the one giving me the most flack for not being his omega. But I wasn't ready for all of that.

"Oh god," I moaned, throwing my head back in pleasure as they hit my erogenous zones.

"Are you going to miss my cock?" asked Ian, his breath on my lips. My breasts bounced up and down as he shoved

160

himself into me one last time. "Fuck, I'm going to knot inside you now."

"Yes, I'm going to miss it," I gasped as I felt the swelling rapidly stretch my pussy. My heart pounded in anticipation for Evan's cock, and soon enough, he was also knotting inside of me. "Oh my god."

"Fuck," groaned Evan, kissing my shoulder. "You're so tight."

They led me towards the sofa, and I wrapped my legs around Ian's waist while Evan settled behind me. It would be at least twenty minutes more with them before I had to leave. The clothes that Sergio had bought for me were packed in bags in the living room, and I tried not to look at them. I didn't want to be overcome with emotion during our last moments together.

Ian looked down at our conjoined privates.

"I'm going to miss touching you like this," he said, rubbing my pussy which was hugging his penis. I couldn't help but clench, and he groaned in pleasure. "Keep doing that, and you're staying another night."

We had lost control this morning when I finished packing up my things. I never intended to get knotted again outside of my heat, but I couldn't help it, and they couldn't either.

The front door suddenly opened, and I quickly looked up, my heart beating hard. It was Sergio standing there, and his eyes narrowed when he saw us.

"I thought she was gone?"

"Serg," I said, breathing hard and trying to wiggle loose of their knots, but I was stuck in place.

"Not yet," breathed Ian.

"You said you were leaving this morning," said Sergio, slamming the door behind him and walking into the house. He dropped his keys onto the kitchen counter and stood there with his arms crossed. His eyes darkened as he saw me skewered between the two men, and his chest heaved up and down from his own arousal.

I didn't realize how much I missed him.

"Sorry, we got carried away, Serg," said Evan, who was rubbing the kinks from my shoulders. "Why are you so mad at us?"

"You know why," he growled, watching me while I leaned my head against Ian's chest. "I'll stay upstairs until you guys take her back to her parents."

"Are you serious?" I said.

"I might lose control," he said, his nostrils flaring at my cherry scent in the air. "Like right about fucking now."

"You won't," I said, then he stalked towards me and touched my chin with his finger.

"What makes you so sure, little omega?" he said.

"Because you didn't lose control last time," I whispered. "You came back to me at the last second. I trust you."

He grunted and stood up over me.

"To see you with my pack's cocks inside you is nearly sending me into a rut," he said.

"Then do it," I challenged. I missed him enough so he could touch me again, but instead, he backed away from me like I was a ticking bomb. Tears rolled down my cheeks. It was unreasonable, and I was angry at myself for crying.

My pussy twitched again over Ian's cock as I saw Sergio's hard-on beneath his pants. He looked worse for wear in a dirty gray shirt and black jeans. His face was unshaven, and his hair unkempt.

"I will see you around, Liv," he said, making his way up the stairs without turning back to look at me.

～

"Let's go," said Evan when I lingered at the front door of their home. I wanted to say goodbye to Sergio one last time, but maybe he was right.

"Alright, I'm coming," I said, slowly turning away from the home and following Ian to the black car. I had to close this chapter of my life forever and start over as fresh as possible with a new pack that didn't know my past.

It was the only way.

As I sat on the passenger side, I felt a little bit sad that Sergio didn't come out to kiss me or at least say bye after everything. Apparently, he didn't care enough, and I had to get over him. Ian reached over, grabbing my thigh while he drove. Evan rode in the backseat, with me cuddling me to him.

"Don't think too hard," said Ian. "Serg will do his own thing, no matter what we tell him."

"He can be a stubborn son of a bitch," said Evan. "But on the bright side, you're finally going to see your family today."

"I am," I said, lighting up at the thought. I missed my family. They were everything to me. After giving Ian my address, I sat back and relaxed while I listened to the music playing in the car.

"I'm sure you're excited about that," said Evan, and I nodded quietly. I was excited, but the innocent light I had before my attack was extinguished. It felt like there was a dark cloud looming over me at all times now.

When we arrived at my family's home, I saw a bunch of cars parked in the driveway.

"Wait, drive slower," I said, quickly looking into the mirror above me to touch up my hair and makeup. I was wearing the short dress that Sergio had bought for me since I had nothing else to wear.

Ian parked the car, and we walked to the house together while Evan carried my bags. Before I could ring the doorbell, my mother flew out the door, hugging me. Her perfume hit my nose, and suddenly, I was overcome with emotion at her familiar scent. Everything about her represented a safer time in my life.

I broke down crying as she hugged me soundlessly.

"Shh, it's okay now, Libby," she said. "You're home now."

"She's here," I heard my fathers saying as they also sprinted out of the house. I opened my tear-stained eyes to see them eying at Ian and Evan.

"They're good," I quickly said. "They saved my life."

"Thank you," said my dad, Caleb, hugging the two alphas. Then my dads hugged me next, and I smiled tearfully. I couldn't believe I was finally home and out of the hellhole.

"Lacy's here too," my mom said, and I saw my cousin hesitantly approaching our little circle.

Her hand was over her belly, and she was biting her lip. I could tell she was pregnant even though she wasn't showing too much yet. *Wow.* A brief thought flashed through my mind that she'd completely forgotten me. I blinked, trying to dispel the thought, and I smiled brightly at her to show no hard feelings.

"Did you miss me?" I said.

"Of course," she said, hugging me, and I hugged her back. "I'm so sorry cousin."

"You did what you had to do," I said, vowing never to tell anyone what truly happened to me. I would just pretend everything was back to normal, and I would force all my past memories of the camp to disappear from my mind.

"I know, but still," she said, tears in her eyes. Her pink lipstick glistened in the sun. "I never wanted to leave you there…"

"Listen, it's fine," I said more firmly. "Let's just never talk about that place again, okay?"

She nodded gratefully, "okay."

"I made food," said my mom. "Let's eat girls. Would you like to join us, Ian and Evan?"

"We have quite a busy day," started Ian, but Evan cut him off.

"Yes, we'd love to join you," said Evan.

As I walked back into my childhood home, arm in arm with my cousin and my mother, I took in the delicious smell of baked bread.

It was so good to be back.

I hadn't realized how much I missed my old life until I walked in. I had felt like a shell of a person for too long, trapped at the camp. Without a family and without a proper home, it had turned me almost soulless.

But now- a new warmth settled inside my heart, and my eyes pricked with tears as I sat at the table with everyone. I was given a new lease on life, and I was going to make sure I made the best of it.

Twenty-Six

OLIVIA

*I*t was dark. The room was always dark as I huddled in my corner.

But the door slammed open, and I jumped, trying to scoot back against the wall until the cold concrete seeped through my skin. I couldn't hide any longer. He lifted me by the hair until I was on my hands and knees.

"Please let me go," I screamed.

"Shush, little Button," said Brett. "You're going to get used to me holding your hair while I fuck you from behind."

"Wake up, Libby. Wake up."

My eyes snapped open, my heart racing from the nightmare. I saw my mother sitting beside me, her hand on my shoulder. My pillow was drenched with tears, and I was sweating bullets.

I was so glad to be awake.

"Sorry," I said, shivering as the remnants of the dream disappeared from my memory. But it would happen again. The memories were always buried deep within me, no matter how hard I tried to forget.

"It's been a week, and you're always crying in your sleep,"

said Mom with sorrow in her eyes. "What happened to you, Libby? Will you ever tell me?"

"Fine," I sighed, closing my eyes. I was always her strong daughter, and I always acted like I had everything under control. But this was too much even for me to bear.

"So what happened?"

"They...violated me at the camp," I said. "Multiple alphas at a time."

"What?!" she said, and I opened my eyes to see her crying. "My baby."

"It's okay now," I said. Every bone in my body ached as I sat up. It always felt like I was perpetually tired all the time ever since coming back home. "I'm okay, Mom."

"Not if you keep having nightmares like this every day," she said, shaking her head. Her long hair had come loose of its bun in her worry.

"I guess," I said, staring at my feet. Damn, I needed to cut my toenails. I'd literally been in bed for so long that I didn't care how I looked.

"I'll set up a therapy appointment for you," my mom said, standing up. "The therapy clinic for omegas who went through trauma. I'll have to ask your father what the name of the clinic is."

"No, Mom," I said, panicking. "I don't need to go there. I'm not crazy."

"Going to therapy doesn't mean you're crazy," she said. "You suffered a lot of pain, and it should help you process."

"Mom, no," I said. "I don't give a fuck. I'm not going."

"Libby," she said, sighing. "There's no need to swear. Then will you at least get out of the house and accept the invite from Lacy?"

My cousin Lacy had invited me to go on a camping trip with her from the voicemails she left me. I ignored the voicemails and her calls because I couldn't be bothered. I didn't feel like talking to anyone, and I needed to rest.

"Fine, I'll make an effort," I said. "As long I don't need to go into therapy."

"Okay," she said, finally letting go of the therapy idea. "But if you ever feel like you need it, I'll set up an appointment right away."

～

LATER THAT MORNING, I sat down at the dining table in my pajamas, about to eat the plate of scrambled eggs my mom had prepared. She had been intent on spoiling me since I got back, and I wasn't complaining. But when the smell hit my nose, I suddenly felt nauseous, and I ran to the garbage, puking out everything.

"Are you okay?" shouted my father, Dravin, who ran into the kitchen.

"What's happening?" said my mother in her usual panicky voice as I wiped my mouth with the paper towel my dad handed me.

"I don't know what just happened," I said, feeling sick at the thought of the eggs.

"Oh no," she said with dread in her tone.

"What, Mom?" I asked, my stomach sinking already at what she was going to tell me. "Actually, don't tell me what you're thinking."

"You might be pregnant," she said.

"I'm not," I said adamantly.

"You didn't get out of bed for a week, and now you're sick," she said, holding a hand to her mouth in horror.

"We'll take care of you," said Dravin. "And you're going to be a grandmother, Jade."

"Shut up," my mom said, rolling her eyes at my dad. "This

isn't a joke. Our daughter is unmated, without a job, and she still hasn't figured out her life."

"Yes, you're right, baby," said Dravin. "But omegas have nothing to worry about. Their alphas take care of them."

"That was a long time ago," my mom sighed. "Now it's hard to find a good alpha these days."

"I'm not pregnant, though," I said, breathing hard as I paced around the living room despite my roiling stomach. I already felt like vomiting again, and panic settled inside me. If I *was* pregnant, what the hell was I going to do with my life?

"Please buy a test for her," Mom said, and my dad immediately left the house, keys in hand.

"I need some space right now," I said, walking to my room.

"Libby, please don't be immature right now."

"I just need time to think about stuff, that's all," I said.

There was no way in hell I was going to take the pregnancy test. I was still plagued by nightmares constantly, and I had come home to a voicemail from Howl's Honor Hospital firing me from my receptionist job. Also, the fact that Sergio hated me weighed heavily on me. I couldn't just easily forget about him.

Picking up a pen and my raggedy notebook full of half-written stories, I flipped through them and stopped upon one that I had particularly enjoyed writing. It was about an omega who had fallen in love with someone outside the island. I wanted to get lost in another person's story right about now. It was thrilling to write about her journey, but I was too shaken to write, so I set the notebook down.

Maybe I *did* need to get out of the house and just go on the damn camping trip with Lacy and my friend Manny. Pulling out my backpack in my very cluttered room, I started throwing in things I'd need for the trip.

Hearing a knock at the door, I got up to unlock it.

"Here you go," said my dad gruffly, handing the pink pregnancy box to me, standing there awkwardly. We'd never had a conversation about me mating alphas or about pregnancy.

"Thanks," I said.

"Let me know when you take it!" screeched my mom from the living room.

"I'm not taking it," I called back, and I heard her sigh of annoyance. Dumping it on my dresser, I resumed packing. I was ready to get out of here for a few days already, despite how much I missed being home because it was suffocating to me now.

I hadn't realized how much I had actually changed, and I was way more impatient with things.

A COUPLE OF DAYS LATER, I walked out of my room, ready to go on the trip with Lacy. I wore my sunglasses already with my backpack slung over my shoulder. Lacy was waiting outside in a van with her pack. I decided to wear something simple- jeans and a blue tank top.

"Did you take the test?" my mom asked as I headed out. She asked me that every day, but I still refused to take the damn test.

"Nope," I said. "I'm not pregnant, Mom. I'll see you when I get back."

"Have fun," she said, her face glowing with happiness at seeing me leave the house. She was so odd sometimes.

"I'll try," I said, giving her a hug. *Who knew what would happen if I ever left the house again?* It was a new kind of paranoia that I had to stop myself from developing. But the fear was still there that I could easily get kidnapped again.

I went outside and saw Lacy all excited with the van door open. The inside was crowded with camping supplies.

"Hey, cuzzo," said Lacy, making room for me in the van as

I flung my backpack on top of the pile. I sat in the middle seat with her while three of her alphas sat in the back row and two at the front. They all started out as her bodyguards, but they had all fallen in love with her during duty.

"How have you been?" I asked Lacy carefully as the van started moving. I hadn't talked to her ever since I got home last week and had been avoiding her calls.

"I'm great," she said. "I would've liked to know how *you'd* been all week. I called you a million times, Liv."

"I know," I said, looking out the window. "I just needed time to process everything."

"Yeah," she sighed sadly. "I never felt at ease since I knew you were still trapped. Every day, I remember you there."

"Listen, we won't talk about it," I said. "I just want to go camping and relax a little. Let's talk about other things, like your singing. How are Ben and Ty?"

I needed to change the subject quickly because I was scared I might blurt out the truth to her about what really happened at the OBC. I didn't want her to know what happened to me or anyone for that matter except for my mother. I felt ashamed, embarrassed, and dirty, like it was my fault it happened. She wouldn't understand since she hadn't gone through anything like I did there.

At the mention of two other males, Ryder growled from the driver's seat.

"Oh, hush," said Lacy, rolling her eyes. "I work with them, and I sleep with you at night, so there is no need to act all territorial now."

I laughed, and soon the mood brightened again. Lacy rested her hand on her belly, and I contemplated asking her if she was pregnant, even though I couldn't tell. But I didn't want to act creepy as hell.

Oh, fuck it.

"Lacy, are you pregnant?"

"I am," she confirmed, looking down.

"Oh, congratulations," I said. "How many months?"

"Two, but there's also something else…"

"Yeah?" I asked, not sure what else could top this news. I was happy for her, but it only made me think of my own possible pregnancy. I really hoped I wasn't pregnant. I still felt sick every morning, but I refused to take the test and be subjected to what reality had to offer.

"I got married too," said Lacy. "Meet my new husbands."

Now that hurt. She went ahead and got married without me being there. Did she even intend to ever come back for me? *What the hell?!*

But I put on a fake smile instead of losing it on her, "I'm really happy for you. You deserve all the happiness in the world. No need to put your life on hold because of me."

Twenty-Seven

OLIVIA

"**W**hy are you setting up your tent so far away?" Lacy asked, following me.

"I don't want to hear any knottings going on," I said, and she blushed furiously.

"God, you don't have to be so gross," she said. "I'll come back when you're less grouchy."

Manny and Adam, whom I considered brothers to me, had also arrived on the trip. We had all grown up together as children, and our mothers were very close, so we were comfortable with each other.

"It's so amazing you're here again," said Manny, helping me with my tent while Adam worked on his tent to share with Manny. "I tried my best with the Royal Pack and all, but they wouldn't pay attention to a sigma like me."

"Wait, are you sure you're a sigma?" I asked.

I was happy for him but also apprehensive since sigmas weren't accepted well into the Howl's Edge community yet. I took a good look at him. Considering his wide shoulders and big-boned structure, I could see that he was a sigma. There weren't many of these types of werewolves on the island, and were shunned in the past as outcasts. They didn't like to be ordered about by authority, which is why his sigma fathers never lived in the city and would rather live on the outskirts of the island.

"Yes," he said, smiling. "Just like my dads, Kodan and Seth. Even though Luke is an alpha, he treats me the same."

"Of course he would," I said, hugging him. "He's your dad too."

But Manny's face suddenly fell, "my beta girlfriend doesn't think it's cool that I'm a sigma, and I could tell she's disgusted by me."

"Aw, Manny, I'm sorry," I said, tucking my hair behind my ear. It was a little windy today despite the sun. "You'll find someone who'll appreciate you. Or maybe she'll come around."

"Highly doubt that," he said. "What's up with you and Lacy? Your tent is so far from hers."

"Nothing," I said. "I just want to be nearer to the trees."

After we finished setting up our tents, we all decided to go on a hike before lunch. I tried to enjoy myself talking to everyone, but I kept to myself. The hurt still settled within me that everyone just forgot about me despite what I'd gone through.

They didn't give a fuck if I died or not.

"You seem quiet today," said Adam when we took a break from walking, and we all sat around on the boulders.

"From what she'd gone through, I don't blame her," said Lacy, speaking for me. I gritted my teeth, sitting there as they talked. But then Lacy addressed me. "Aren't you glad you came on this trip with me? Your mom thought it would be a good idea for me to take you out of the house."

"My mom?" I asked, taken aback. Annoyance swirled through me that she'd been talking to my mom behind my back.

"Yeah, she called me and said it would be a good idea for us to do something," said Lacy.

"So you did all this for me?"

"Well...yeah, but I also wanted to have fun," she said, smiling and not at all aware that I was fuming by now.

"So whatever my mom says, you'll just do it? Without talking to me first?"

"Well, I know what you've been through," she said sheepishly.

At that, I shot up from my seat, breathing rapidly. "You don't have a clue what happened to me. None of you have a fucking clue what I went through! Why don't you all stop pretending to be my friends and go back to your fucking lives?"

"Whoa, whoa," said Adam, getting up and touching my arm, but I shook him off, backing away. Lacy sat there silently with a shocked look on her face, her eyes wide and filled with tears.

"I didn't mean for..." she started to say, but I cut her off while Adam and Manny watched us.

"I need to be alone," I snapped, walking off into the trees away from all of them. Then I turned back, "Don't wait for me! Go home if you want. I'll get home on my own."

"Olivia," said Lacy, trying to come after me, but I held up a hand.

"Just don't," I said. "How could you have a whole wedding without me there? You didn't give two fucks if I was left at the camp, did you?"

"I tried," she said. "I promise you I did. I told myself you would be fine until help arrived."

"No, I wasn't fine," I retorted. "I was raped. Not once or twice but multiple times and with multiple alphas. How about you do me a favor and leave?"

"Oh my god, I'm so fucking sorry," she said, tears in her eyes now. "Olivia, please."

"I'm serious," I said, turning my gaze to trees before me. "I can't talk to you. I can't even look at you right now. Maybe one day I'll get over it, but today's not the day."

"I'm so sorry," she said, openly sobbing. "I knew this would happen. I begged my alphas, but no one would go back or even let me."

I didn't give a fuck right now. As I stalked off, my pulse thundered in my head, and my heart was pounding hard. I couldn't think straight right now. I couldn't think at all as I walked farther and farther away from the camp.

~

Sergio

I PARKED at Olivia's house just like I did every evening. I would watch her through her bedroom window just to make sure she was okay every night.

Ian and Evan had no idea of my extracurricular activity, which was watching her at night.

But she wasn't here today, and I was starting to get worried.

She wasn't laying in her bed all day, in her pajamas, and she wasn't pacing around anxiously, biting her nails with a pen in hand. *Where could she have gone?* I knew she wasn't in the state of mind to go anywhere, and it was already the end of the day.

Getting out of my car, I walked towards the house.

I took in a deep breath before knocking on the front door. I had to think of something quick to say.

But the door opened, and her mother stood there with a happy smile on her face. I knew it was her mother because of the same oval-shaped eye structure that Liv had and her dark hair.

"Hello, how can I help you?" she asked.

"I know we haven't met yet," I said, sticking out my hand. "But I was one of the alphas who helped rescue your daughter from the OBC."

She shook my hand.

"That horrible place," she sighed. "Thank you for saving my daughter. You must be Sergio, that Ian was telling me about."

"You have a good memory," I said, smiling.

"Come inside, please," she said, and I followed her into her home. Two of her alphas were sitting on the couch, conversing, and one in the kitchen. They stopped talking upon seeing me.

"Who's this?" asked one of them gruffly, standing in front of his omega. "Jade, you can't just let anyone in."

"It's okay, Caleb," she said hastily. "This is Sergio."

"Hello, Sergio," said Caleb, immediately shaking my hand with an iron grip, and upon releasing my hand, my fingers nearly fell off. "It's nice to meet you, Sergio. What can we do for you?"

"I wanted to check on Olivia," I said, getting straight to the point. I was worried about her.

"She's off on a hiking trip with her friends," said her mother, and I raised my eyebrows perplexed. *What would she be doing out camping right now?*

"I'm glad she's out enjoying herself," I said. It was better than her laying in bed all day like she usually did, and it hurt me to see her that way.

"We're hoping it'll help her," she said.

"Are you mated to an omega yet?" Caleb asked me, business-like. "I run a dating agency."

"No, I'm not mated," I said. "And not interested."

"But interested in my daughter? Hopefully, the baby isn't yours then," he said.

"What baby?" I asked in alarm, sitting up straighter on the couch. "Is she pregnant?"

"We think she is, but she refuses to take a pregnancy test," her mom sighed, and she looked annoyed at her husband. "Caleb, you don't have to tell the whole world about it."

"Just checking to see if he's the father," he growled, watching me closely.

"Listen, I have no idea about this," I said, my heart pounding faster. She could be pregnant with *my* baby. "Where exactly did she go? I need to find her."

"Howl's Mount Park," said Caleb, and Jade glared at him.

"Why are you telling him everything?"

"He's our daughter's mate," said Caleb with a smirk, leaning back on the couch. "I can tell he cares deeply for her, and he'll do anything for her. Isn't that right, Sergio?"

"I don't know about us being mates," I said, breathing hard at the thought of Olivia being my omega. He was a matchmaker and could probably sense it. But I wasn't going to give him that satisfaction. "But I *do* care for her, and I want to make sure she's safe."

"It was your scent outside our home ever since she got back, isn't that right?"

Fuck. He knew I was the creeper alpha. No wonder he freaked out on his wife for bringing me into their home.

"Yes...it was."

I stood up from the couch, not sure if he was going to punch me or straight up kick me out of the house. I deserved it for breaking up with their daughter. *Had Liv told them anything about us?*

"Go after her son. You have my blessings," said Caleb, winking at me.

"Caleb, what are you doing?" said Jade indignantly. "You can't do this to our daughter. She has a say, too."

"I'm not going to do anything to her," I reassured her, heading to the door. "I just want to check on her."

"Please keep my daughter safe," said Jade, following me to the door. Then, in a quieter voice. "Do you think it could be *your* baby?"

"I don't know," I said, sweat running down my back.

"What? Were you part of the group who hurt her?" she asked, eyes flashing.

"No," I said vehemently. "She went into heat after we saved her life. Did she tell you that?"

"She didn't," she said, shaking her head. "Sorry for thinking you'd hurt her. Have a good night."

"It's okay," I said. "You didn't know the whole story."

With that, I headed out the door, perplexed by Liv's parents. No wonder she stayed in her room all day depressed. I was going to find her and make sure she was okay. And she could be carrying my child in her belly right now.

Hopping into my car, I went in the general direction of the park that Caleb had mentioned and thought about Liv as I drove.

I thought about her cherry lips and scent. Her curly black hair fanning out under my chin when she rested her head on my chest. I missed everything about her, and I couldn't wait to talk to her.

I needed her to know how I truly felt and how I would never let her go ever again.

Twenty-Eight

OLIVIA

After walking for several hours, occasionally vomiting into bushes- I stumbled into a dark cave for some shelter. It had gotten dark outside, and fear went through me upon entering the cave. *Shit, I had gone too far from the camp.* Ahead of me was a cliff, so I decided to stop and rest here.

Sitting in the cave was terrifying. I couldn't see anything in the dark, and panic settled within me.

But the longer I sat there, the more I was lost to the darkness.

"No, no, no," I said out loud as memories started to surface again. Memories of the OBC. Memories of Brett and the sweaty alphas. "No!"

I ran out of the cave and breathed in deeply when I looked up at the moon, which barely peeked through the trees. Tears flowed down my cheeks as I stood there staring at the cliff.

I could just end it all.

Make all my memories disappear.

My feet seemed to move by themselves toward the edge, and my heart pumped wildly as tears streamed down my face.

Nobody gave a fuck about me. I was just a breeding tool for alphas.

And maybe I was. I was just a toy for the alphas.

I stood at the edge of the cliff, looking down at the swirl of darkness that would end me. The peace of no more worrying.

I held a hand to my belly, suddenly feeling a flutter within me. And chills went through me.

At that moment, I knew I was carrying a baby within me. *Was it fair to him that I might end my life right now? And his life?*

No, no I couldn't do this.

Letting out a long breath, I turned around on wobbly legs. I couldn't believe I almost gave in to the dark. My heart was beating wildly in my chest, from my attempt.

But I suddenly slipped on the edge.

I screamed as I felt myself start to fall in the air, and I automatically reached out to grab the edge, but instead, my hand wrapped around someone else's.

The hand quickly pulled me up mid-air, setting me on the ground.

"Olivia," barked a deep male voice.

I looked up to see Sergio standing there as he gripped my hand in his. His hair flew back in the wind as he glared at me with pity in his eyes.

Shit.

"Hey," I said, crossing my arms over my chest. "Nice to see you're back to knot me some more. Didn't you get enough of me, like you said?"

"I'm not here to knot you," he growled. "What are you doing, trying to kill yourself, Olivia?!"

My pulse was thundering in my ears, and tears were streaming down my face. I couldn't move, and I was shaking uncontrollably. Sergio wrapped me in a hug, and I sunk into his body, allowing his alpha warmth to envelop me. My body shuddered as I sobbed into his chest, and he purred into my neck.

"I...I couldn't stop myself," I said in a shaky voice as he rubbed my back.

"Shh, Liv," he purred. "You can tell me in a few moments when you've calmed down. But you're going to tell me everything, alright?"

I nodded against his chest, and he let out a grunt of satisfaction. We stood there for a few minutes while he held me tight, and memories of what I did ran through my mind. I couldn't believe I just tried to end my life.

But the despair hadn't left me.

The only thing that stopped me at the last minute was the baby in my belly. The baby had let me know that he was there, and I sobbed harder at the realization.

"I almost killed him," I hiccuped.

"Who?"

"My baby," I said.

Sergio slowly released me and cupped my face in his hands. He wiped away my tears with his thumbs.

"Well, you didn't," he said. "Thank fuck that I came in time. I would have lost you forever. Let's sit you down somewhere while I build a fire for us."

"Okay," I said, walking with trembling legs towards the cave, but then I stopped. "Let's go somewhere else."

It felt nice to have Sergio by my side as we walked between the trees, looking for a spot to settle for the night. He took care of me, brushing away the twigs from my shirt and offering to carry me half the time. My feet were sore, but I didn't want to accept his offer. I had no idea why he was even here. I needed to know why the hell he came back looking for me when he hadn't cared before when I left his home.

Locating a cozy spot in front of a small riverbed, I sat on a boulder as he collected whatever he could to build a fire. It was colder out here than on the mainland, so I hugged myself, shivering as I watched Sergio gather up wood in a small pile before me.

Soon, he had a raging fire going, and he scooped me up in his arms, surrounding me in his warmth once again as we watched the fire together.

Something about sitting on his lap wrapped between his arms, put a sense of safety and security within me.

"You've been through a lot today, babe," he said in a low voice next to my ear. "Do you mind telling me how you got separated from everyone?"

I really didn't feel like explaining myself, but he had saved my life after all.

"We got into a fight," I said simply, without going into details. He didn't need to hear all the details. "I walked away, that's all. Then I slipped on the edge of the cliff."

"Are you sure you just 'slipped'?" he interrogated, pressing his chin to my shoulder. I sighed, and I knew there was no way I could avoid telling him the truth.

"I wanted to end it at first," I said. "Then I changed my mind, and I slipped."

He was probably thinking that I was a crazy, suicidal omega hell-bent on hurting myself. I shrank while sitting on his lap, trying not to look at him.

"Why did you want to end it, little omega?" he asked. His gentle voice nearly had me crying again. "So many people care about you. Especially your parents."

"The memories of getting violated were too much," I said. "I couldn't handle it anymore."

"You're strong," he said, and I closed my eyes, trying not to cry. "You were strong the entire time at the OBC, and you'll be strong during your healing process. Don't forget that."

"Thank you," I whispered.

"Don't give up hope," he said. "For yourself, your family. And for...me."

My stomach flipped at his last sentence. I didn't know what he meant by that, but it would be something I'd think about tonight.

"Do you really care about me?" I asked.

"Let's just say that I never want to leave your side again," said Sergio. "Will you be my omega?"

"Is it because I might be pregnant?" I said, wondering why he didn't look more surprised at the possibility.

"No," he said. "I went to your house every day to check on you. I watched you sleep."

"What?" I said, shocked.

I tried to remember if I had ever closed the curtain at night, and I knew I hadn't because I loved the moonlight. I hated being in absolute darkness.

"Yes, I know. I'm sorry," he said. "I just wanted to make sure you were safe. But instead of doing that anymore, you could just be mine."

"I don't even know you," I sighed. "Like anything personal about you."

"We could go on dates?" he suggested, and my face broke into a smile. "What would you like to know about me?"

"How did you end up at the OBC?" I started, turning on his lap to face him. I watched his eyes glaze over in memory.

"I lived with a foster family," he said. "I don't really like talking about it, but I care about you. So here goes."

"Okay."

"I found a letter in my mother's room," he said. "A letter from my real mother, and I confronted my foster mom about it. She eventually confessed that I came from the omega breeding camp. From there, my search for my real mother started."

"Oh wow."

"I signed up with the Royal Pack to be a spy at the camp since many alphas were either in cahoots with Henry or they were too afraid to stand up to their own kind."

"Did you find her?"

"I did not," he said, letting out a long breath laced with emotion. "For years, I stayed at the OBC, hoping to find her, but I had no luck. I asked for Sylvia everywhere I went, and nothing."

The name struck a memory within me. The memory of Krissy mentioning something about an older lady named Sylvia who died there. My breath caught, and I debated whether or not to mention it.

"I think I might know what happened to her," I said. "It might not be her, though."

"What happened?" he asked with bated breath. "Tell me."

"The girls in the birthing building told me there was an older lady named Sylvia who died," I said, and tears shone in his eyes. "I'm so sorry, Sergio."

"It was bound to happen to her," he said finally. "I wished to have seen her just once. To let her know that I'm okay."

We held each other in front of the fire, lost in our own thoughts. I felt bad that he hadn't seen his real mother and that he was a direct victim of Henry's conniving plans.

"I hate Henry," I said. "I hope they catch him."

"You have no idea how much I despise him," he said. "He's a sick bastard, intent on destroying families to fit his vision of Howl's Edge."

"Good riddance to him, though," I said, and suddenly, Sergio lifted my chin as I sat sideways on his lap. My heart thumped as we gazed into each other's eyes, and then he captured my lips hungrily with his.

And I kissed him back with equal force. My heart pounded hard as we kissed in front of the fire, hungry for each other. I clenched my thighs as my scent floated around us.

"I'm sorry," he breathed against my lips. "I just wanted to taste one more time."

"Don't be," I whispered. "I want it too."

His eyes darkened, and my stomach clenched once again in arousal. Suddenly, we were ripping each other's clothes off. I was desperate to feel his warm alpha skin against mine again. I wanted to be rutted one more time even though I hadn't committed to him that I was his omega.

Completely naked before the fire, he spread my legs while I lay on my back. He was grunting on top of me as he gripped his cock in his hand. Shuddering under his gaze, I spread my naked thighs wider and circled my pussy with my finger.

"Fuck, keep doing that, baby," he breathed, gripping his dick while he watched me. I rubbed my pussy in circles, getting horny the more he watched me. Slick covered my fingers as I added pressure onto my clit. "Is that how you please yourself in secret? Show Daddy Alpha."

"Okay," I moaned as I rubbed myself harder, flicking my clitoris in front of him. "Please, I want you inside of me. Daddy Alpha."

"Good girl," he groaned, pushing the tip of his cock against my entrance. "Keep touching yourself while I rut you. Be a good girl and rub your clit for me."

"Oh," I gasped as he pushed his length inside me. I lifted my hips to meet his thrusts, enjoying how his cock spread me further with each thrust. "It feels so good, Daddy Alpha."

"Don't stop rubbing your little clit," he warned, and I resumed touching myself as he pounded inside me. I tried to keep my finger directly over my clit, but his thrusts bounced me around too much. Pressing around my clit in circles, I rubbed harder until I could feel my stomach clenching.

"I'm about to...," I gasped, feeling the crescendo of an orgasm take me over. I dropped my hand, my legs shaking as he continued to thrust into my pussy.

"Fuck," he groaned, pushing into me one last time. His cock stretched me as he kissed me furiously all over my neck, and I felt the stream of his liquid flow inside of me. His lips pressed all over my breasts until my chest was heaving in arousal again. "I love you, Liv."

"I love you too," I whispered, unable to stop myself from saying it. It was an overwhelming feeling that just felt right to me. I was scared, but after being on the edge of death, I didn't care anymore.

"I will never leave you again," he promised, kissing me on the lips as his penis swelled, knotting me to him. "I promise to protect you with everything I have to give. I am yours, and my pack is yours. Forever."

Twenty-Nine

OLIVIA

The next day, Sergio parked in front of my parent's house. I had argued with him for the last ten minutes of the drive not to come inside with me, but he was insistent on walking me to my room.

I knew my parents were worried sick about where I was, and might blame it on Sergio.

"Are you sure you want to come inside with me?" I asked, twirling my fingers on my lap.

"Yes," he said stubbornly, turning off the engine. "Everywhere you go, I'll make sure you're safe."

"I'm safe with my parents," I said, rolling my eyes.

"I'll take the heat for any blame."

"I guess I don't have much of a choice now, do I?" I asked, secretly pleased that I didn't have to say goodbye to him just yet. I hadn't agreed to be his omega yet, even though I confessed my feelings to him last night by the fire.

I felt dirty and filthy after my long hike in the mountains yesterday. I was hoping to quickly shower and see Sergio when I was clean, but we both walked to the door. I rang the doorbell, and it seemed like a couple of minutes before the door opened.

"Olivia," my mother said, her arms crossed. I could tell she was upset. "I tried calling you over and over. Lacy had no idea where you were either."

"Sorry, Mom," I sighed.

"She got lost in the woods," said Sergio, coming to my defense. "And I found her alone in a cave."

"Oh no," said Mom, grabbing my face and inspecting my eyes. "Come inside, both of you. This house is yours now, too, Sergio. You've saved my daughter way too many times to count."

I was grateful not to see any of my alpha fathers around since I didn't want to be interrogated right now as I headed to my room. Sergio followed me and sat at the edge of my bed while I locked the door.

It felt odd to have him in here. His presence made my childhood room feel so small. He rested his elbows on his thighs, studying me.

"I came here for a different reason," he whispered, and my heart leaped.

"What for?" I asked, grabbing my towel from the rack next to the door.

"You need to take the pregnancy test," he said.

"Not today," I sighed, looking at the pink box on my dresser. I had grown to hate that little box and avoided it like the plague.

"I can't leave until you do, Liv," he said, licking his lips. "I have to know."

"Fine, let me shower first," I said. I started walking to the bathroom connected to my room, and he started removing his muddy white shirt. "What are you doing?"

"Joining you," he said gruffly.

"And who gave you permission?" I said, stripping off my

clothes. Then, in a harsh whisper, "My mom is in the next room. We can't do this here!"

"If you're my omega, who's going to stop us?" he whispered in my ear, his sideburns brushing against my neck, and I turned to putty in his arms. My inner omega couldn't help but respond immediately to his alpha pheromones.

I tried to be as quiet as possible in the shower, but I knew my mom would be suspicious of why the shower was on while Sergio was here.

Oh well, I'd have to come up with a good excuse.

I couldn't help but wrap my arms around his neck as he lifted me up while we stood under the powerful stream of water. He pressed his nose into the crook of my neck and inhaled deeply.

"I love your scent, Olivia," he said, pressing kisses all across my collarbone.

My heart pumped faster at his words, enjoying the way his warm lips caressed my skin. I gripped his strong, muscular arms so I didn't slip down as I wrapped my legs around his waist. Our lips met, and instead of showering, we kissed while the water dampened my hair from the back. We pulled away, our faces dripping and wet.

"Your kisses are so good," I whispered, and his eyebrows rose.

"Better than Ian and Evan?"

"I'm not answering that," I said quickly, and he chuckled softly. He gently set me down and grabbed my pink loofah that I had hanging above me.

"Ready to be scrubbed down, my dirty little omega?" he asked, his lips pulled up in a one-sided smile as he gazed at me with darkened eyes. "Are you going to let Daddy Alpha wash your ass?"

I could already feel the slick dripping between my legs while he slowly washed my breasts first, covering me in bubbles. I was facing him while the water gushed over us from behind. My pussy throbbed with anticipation, and my heart pounded hard as he washed my belly next, the muscles on his arms covered with short black hair flexing as he concentrated on me.

He paused, allowing the water to wash the soap off my breasts. Then he quickly took my left breast into his mouth, sucking on my nipple while his hand slid between my legs.

Oh my god.

I didn't realize how horny I'd get when he sucked me like that. Every fiber in my body came alive. I gasped, leaning against the wall of the shower as he sucked on my nipple and started rubbing my pussy with his bare hands. His eyes were closed, and he seemed to be in a different world as he rubbed between my folds. Slick seeped from my pussy, mixing with the water the more he sucked on my breast like that.

Gripping his hair, I arched my chest and widened my legs to allow him easier access to me. His eyes were still closed, and I felt freer somehow. My chest rose and fell with fast breaths as I felt my belly contracting with my incoming orgasm.

Then he suddenly slipped his finger inside me, thrusting into my pussy.

Still gripping his hair, he released my swollen nipple and kissed down my belly until he was kneeling before me. He turned his head upwards.

"Sit on my face," he commanded.

"Oh, are you serious?" I asked, scared. I wasn't even sure why I was nervous, but I'd never done anything like this before.

"Yes."

Breathing hard, I took a step forward until his head was trapped between my thick thighs. Then I lowered myself over him, feeling his tongue bury itself into my pussy. I moaned, and I could hear him groaning in pleasure.

"I don't want to put all my weight on you," I said, worried I'd suffocate him.

"Do it," he said, his tone pleading instead of commanding this time. "I want to feel you. Please punish me for leaving you, honey."

"I don't punish people," I said uncertainly.

"Please, mi amor."

I suddenly mashed my pussy over his face, grinding on him furiously. His tongue swirled inside me as I heard him struggling to breathe, and my face turned red. I tried to lighten my weight, but he gripped my hips and kept me sitting on his face.

He sucked on my clit, and I gripped his shoulders as I felt the sensation. His lips tightened around my clit, sucking harder and harder.

Until I climaxed all over his face.

I could hardly take a breath from how powerful it was as I held onto him. My fingers dug into his skin, and I cried out when I felt another orgasm hit me as he continued to suck.

"Fuck," he said. "You taste so good, baby."

Sergio

MY DICK WAS hard as fuck as I sucked her juices. I was trapped under her pussy like I dreamt of. Her pussy quivered over my tongue as I licked her sweet slick.

Her little clit peeked out again, and I quickly rubbed my nose over it as I pressed my tongue deep into her pussy.

"Are you done?" she gasped.

"Shh, your mom will hear," I said, purring against her pussy, and she jumped. The vibrations of my purr caused her pussy to clench one more time, and she moaned uncontrollably, trying to pull away from my face. But I gripped her thighs, slamming her pussy over my face as I drank ravenously like a thirsty animal.

She tasted so good. So divine. She was mine.

"Please, I'm done," she yelped as I swiped my tongue one more time over her clit. I reluctantly released her thighs, and I helped her as she stood on trembling legs. But I wasn't done.

"Bend down, little omega," I said. Her face turned pink, and she was still gasping from her orgasm. I couldn't help but kiss her on the mouth before she obeyed my command. Her soft lips were plump under mine as she tasted herself on my lips. "Do you see why I don't get enough of your pussy?"

She licked her lips experimentally.

"Oh, stop," she said, blushing furiously. But her pulse rate increased, and her breasts were swollen. I pinched her nipples, and she cried out, dropping her head back. Then I released her breasts and turned her around by her shoulders.

"Bend down so I can see your ass," I instructed, she hesitated.

I wasn't going to force her. Not at all, so I watched her.

She slowly bent down for me and gripping the loofah in my hand, I washed between her crack. Up and down, I washed as I stared at her plump bottom, trembling before me. I pressed the material deeper between her cheeks, watching as her clit began to peek out in arousal.

Her pussy clenched the harder I rubbed her ass. I wanted to see her asshole.

Dropping the loofah, I rinsed off the soap and gently spread her cheeks apart as I took a good look at her bottom. Her asshole was quivering as I gazed upon it. I pressed my face between her cheeks and licked around her anus, watching her hole clench.

"What are you doing?" she asked, shocked as she clamped up.

"Just want to taste my omega," I said, licking around and

around her small hole. "Soon, you're going to take Daddy Alpha's cock inside your small hole. Are you going to let him do that?"

"Yes," she said, holding onto the wall for balance when I jammed the tip of my tongue into her ass. I thrust my tongue deeper inside her, feeling her anal walls clench around my tongue. While my tongue explored, I pushed a finger into her pussy to feel her warmth. "This is so crazy, but god, it feels so good at the same time."

"Mhm," I said, pulling out from her ass, squeezing her cheeks firmly. "Now, let's see if you're pregnant. We've spent enough time in here fooling around. Are you going to take the test, little omega?"

"I don't want to," she whined, and I squeezed her cheeks again. I knew she wanted to annoy me on purpose, and I smiled with amusement while she wasn't looking at me. Jamming my tongue into her ass again, she yelped, and I felt a squirt of her slick onto my finger from her pussy. "Okay, fine. I'll take it."

"Good girl," I breathed against her ass. I blew air onto her quivering little hole, and she jumped again. "Can't wait to see if I'm going to be a father."

Thirty

OLIVIA

"I'm taking it," I conceded when he handed me the test. "Aren't you going to leave?"

"I want to watch you," said Sergio, who stood in front of the closed bathroom door, his arms crossed in front of him. His penis was erect, and I couldn't help but gaze at the full size of it.

"Fine, you'll just get disgusted," I said, sitting on the toilet naked from my shower. I pretended he wasn't there as I placed the stick under the stream of my pee. He took the stick from me and placed the cap over it. "It looks like you've done this before."

"I've read the instructions," he said shortly, placing the stick on the sink as I wiped myself. "We'll leave it here until the timer goes off."

"Fine by me," I said. "I don't even want to look at it."

I washed my hands and proceeded to look for an extra towel for him as we entered my room. Handing him a towel, I wondered if I was really pregnant. I had the innate feeling at the cliff, but maybe it was just my imagination. I put on a fresh pair of underwear, jeans, and a shirt after applying lotion. I turned to see him dressed in just his pants.

He was shirtless, and he looked hot as fuck standing like that in the middle of my room. If he walked out like that, my mom would definitely know something was up.

"Yeah, I know," he said, looking down at bare chest. "I mainly showered with you, just so I can touch you before I leave."

I smiled at his confession as I sat on my bed cross-legged. I was hungry as hell, and the smell of my mom's cooking made my stomach growl. Suddenly, the timer went off, and my appetite took a nose-dive.

"You can look at it first," I said.

He went into the bathroom, and I watched him pick it up. I looked away so I didn't see what his facial expression would reveal. Then when I saw him kneel before me on the edge of the bed, I was freaking out.

My heart thundered in my ears, and my hands shook as he silently handed me the test while kissing my belly. There was a big blue plus sign clear as day on it.

"You're pregnant," he growled.

"It must be a mistake," I said, panicking as the test dropped to the floor because my hands were shaking so much. It was like a thunderbolt crashed through the sky, the news shaking me to the core.

"Not at all," said Sergio. "Why are you so scared, Liv?"

"I never imagined getting pregnant," I said. "I wanted to have a baby with a pack who cares about me."

"And you have that," said Sergio, looking at me with warmth in his eyes. "How about we go on a lunch date tomorrow with my pack?"

"I know you feel obligated, but I can take care of myself and the baby," I said. "Seriously."

"Even if you weren't pregnant, I want you," he said.

"Believe it or not, I can't bear to even leave you right now. How about that lunch date?"

"Fine," I said, sighing.

Then I looked at his face and smiled. A realization settled inside me when I looked into his eyes. He would do anything for me, and warmth poured into my soul. Leaning down, I grasped his face and kissed him, to his shock.

"Hm, what was that for?" he asked with a grin.

"I just felt like it," I said. "A burst of...of love, I guess."

He breathed deeply, raising himself onto my bed and pulling me into a hug. I could feel his chest puffing proudly beneath me as he absorbed my scent around us.

"I love you, Liv. More than you'll ever know."

Tears burned at my eyes and slid down my cheeks as I cuddled into his warmth. Then I smelt his shirt.

"I love you too, Serg, but you need to go before my mom freaks out," I said, pulling away. His eyes danced with amusement at my words.

"Alright, alright," he said, lifting his hands. "I'm going to head out now. I'll see you tomorrow, love."

When he left my bedroom, I sat there for a moment, listening to him talking to my mom. I sat there for a moment, thinking about how I nearly killed myself yesterday, and if Sergio hadn't caught me, I wouldn't be here. I took deep breaths to calm my panicked breathing.

Maybe I needed some help.

THE NEXT DAY, I couldn't believe I was sitting in group therapy for traumatized omegas.

"Why don't you all start by introducing yourselves?" the therapist said as I sat in the circle of chairs.

I had gotten the information about this facility during

dinner with my mom, to which she was super excited about me going. The therapist was a tall omega who displayed the mark of the claw proudly on her shoulder as she sat amongst us in the circle. Her long brown hair was tied into a ponytail, and she looked at each of us with kind eyes.

"My goal is to make sure you are comfortable telling your story. And the more you talk about it, the better you'll feel when it no longer has control over you to stay silent."

I sat there listening to the omegas' stories as they each talked about being sold at the auction years ago or having been violated by an alpha family member. When I heard the mention of an omega breeding camp, I quickly looked up and was shocked to see Reyna sitting there.

"I really don't want to talk about it, but I need to heal to have a normal life," said Reyna. "When I was just a teen, I hired a bodyguard because my family was psychotic. All they could talk about was making sure I'd sell for a nice price at the auctions."

She paused, looking down with her lips trembling. My heart went out to her, knowing where this story was going since she eventually ended up at the OBC.

"You're doing great," said the therapist, smiling at her. "Don't let it control you."

"Instead of the auctions, they found a better deal," said Reyna. "To sell me to Henry. The psychotic bastard who kept a bunch of omegas to make babies for him, so my uncle kidnapped me."

I listened, as did all the other omegas, who were in shocked silence as she explained the brutality in detail. I remembered myself, night after night, waiting for the alphas to arrive and then wishing the time would go by faster while they took me. I didn't realize my eyes were shut tight at the memories until the therapist called on me next.

"Olivia, what memories are you grappling with?" asked the therapist.

"Everything she's saying about the OBC is true," I gasped out, opening my eyes. The omega next to me handed a tissue to me. "Thank you."

"What memories does it trigger in you?" asked the therapist.

"I don't want to talk about it," I said, breathing hard as I stared at my sneakers.

"Remember, it's the only way to heal."

"I said I don't want to talk," I snapped, breathing hard. "Do you just want to hear about me getting raped over and over again by a sick alpha and his buddies? It's the same story, just like the rest of these ladies."

Surprisingly, saying it out loud shed the weight of its power over me. And I began to breathe a little easier despite the heavy weight on my chest.

"You have experienced a tremendous amount of pain," said the therapist. "My goal is to help you, not attack you."

I nodded silently, blowing my nose into the tissue.

"I think I'm done for now," I said, getting up. I walked away from there, embarrassed to death of snapping at the therapist. I wish I hadn't done that. When I got outside, I walked to my car, but before I could unlock the door, a voice stopped me.

"Olivia," said a rough female's voice.

I turned and saw that Reyna had followed me out here.

"Hey Reyna," I said, my hand on the door handle. "It's cool seeing you here."

"Why don't you come back and finish the session?" she asked. "Don't be impatient."

"I just embarrassed myself," I said, shaking my head and squeezing the car keys. "I'm never going back there again."

"You didn't embarrass yourself," she said. "I did the same thing at first."

"You did?"

"I sure did," she replied, smiling. I noticed she looked a lot cleaner and taken care of. Her teeth were whiter now, and she looked more distinguished in her black blazer with jeans. "I was a complete brat. You're better than me, Olivia."

I sighed and shoved my keys back into my purse. I had gone through the horror Reyna had, but she'd been suffering for far longer than myself.

"Alright," I said. "I'll give it one more try."

Thirty-One

OLIVIA

Days later, I woke up for the first time without nightmares.

Opening my eyes, my hand automatically went to my belly, imagining the growing baby inside of me.

The therapy sessions seemed to be helping, in addition to going out on lunches and dinners with Sergio, Ian, and Evan. During yesterday's group therapy session, I broke down discussing my fears and telling them I was pregnant.

Everyone congratulated me despite not knowing who the father was. I was freaking out about being pregnant every day since I officially found out. But every morning, it had gotten easier to accept that I'd love the baby despite who his father was. Sometimes, I would envision myself with Sergio's pack and our child running around the house. The image would stay with me at night until I was comfortable with the idea and even excited.

Today I was planning to visit a museum with Sergio, Ian and Evan.

I was excited to go, and I had carefully picked out my outfit last night after my therapy session. Every day, my life was slowly repairing itself, and I knew one day I'd have to fix my relationship with Lacy.

After showering and brushing my teeth, I took my time getting ready in a cute dress that I would spend the day in around the island with my pack.

My pack.

I smiled, liking the sound of that as I applied makeup. Hearing a knock at the door, I went to open it, and my mom stood there while clutching a romance book in her hand with rollers in her hair.

"Yes, Mom?"

"Aww, you so look cute," she said. "There's someone in the living room for you."

Wondering if my alphas had come for me already, I headed down the stairs and into the living room. Upon seeing who it was, my blood ran cold.

It was Brett sitting there like he owned the place. He sat on the couch, knees spread, trying to show his dominance.

"What are you doing here?" I asked sharply, feeling my heart beat a mile a minute. This was a shock to me, and I wasn't prepared to see him there. I thought he had been killed or gone to prison with the rest of the alpha handlers.

I stood there petrified.

"I just want to talk to you," he said, smiling. The familiar evil smile that made my stomach hurt, knowing what was coming. He knew I was scared, and I needed to take him out of the house before he hurt my mother.

"Who's that?" my mom asked.

"No one, just an old friend," I said hastily, trying to control my breathing. "We can talk outside."

Brett smiled as if he had won, and he opened the door for me as we walked outside.

"I came to make you a proposal," he said, sniffing the air strongly for my scent.

"You don't scare me anymore," I said loudly, trying to force some bravery to scare him off. Deep down, I was trembling like a leaf, forgetting everything I learned in therapy.

My legs were like jello, and I was the scared omega I was back at the OBC.

"You're going to be my omega," he said. "It looks like alphas haven't scooped you up yet. Would you like to be my omega? I miss you, Button."

"No thanks," I said quickly. "I'm taken already."

"But they haven't marked you yet," he said, touching my neck and I cringed. He noticed my look of disgust. "Why are you acting like this?"

"You know why," I hissed. "You raped me."

"That's an exaggeration," he said, coming closer to me. "You enjoyed every second of it. I can still remember your moans. Come with me."

"I'm not yours!" I shouted, backing away from him.

But he quickly scooped me up, and I screamed as I punched him in the back. I kicked as hard as I could while panic streamed through every nerve of my body. I heard him grunt in pain as he quickly shoved me into the backseat of his car and shut the door.

Before I could open the door, he hopped into the driver's seat and took off. For a moment, I froze in terror.

The car was moving at top speed.

Shoving the door open, my heart pounded fast as I looked at the rushing road beneath. Fuck, I was pregnant.

"Close the door!" roared Brett with the alpha bark in his voice.

Instead, I jumped out.

Pain hit my body.

I rolled around and around on the hard asphalt ground, trying to protect my belly with my arms. When I finally stopped rolling, dizziness hit me when I opened my eyes. And the first thing I saw was Brett looming over me, his eyes flashing with red fury.

"Asshole!" I screamed as he reached out to grab my arms.

Before he could do that, I saw him being thrown against a tree.

I looked around me, seeing Sergio, Ian, and Evan standing around me protectively with me in the middle.

My body hurt as I stumbled to my feet and brushed off the dirt from my dress. We were off the road as the cars zoomed by. Brett's head lolled against the trunk of the tree, and I watched as Evan kicked him repeatedly in the ribs.

"Fucker," screamed Ian, who was kneeling and punching him repeatedly in the face. Brett weakly fought back, but he was no match for three young virile alphas who had the upper hand. "Believe me that you'll never touch a hair on our omega's head ever again."

I watched as they continued to beat him up mercilessly. Brett turned his head towards me. He opened his mouth, which frothed with blood, trying to say something to me.

"Guys, that's enough," I said, weakly walking towards them with every limb in my body aching. "Don't kill him. Call the police."

I knelt in front of him next to Ian.

"My omega," mumbled Brett, crazy-eyed as he gazed at me.

"I will *never* be your omega," I screamed in his face. Then in a calmer tone, as I gripped his cock. "You will never hurt me again. In fact, you'll never hurt anyone else ever again."

His eyes bugged with panic when I yanked at it, and he yelled through his pain. I released him as the police approached us.

"Ma'am, step back," the delta officers commanded.

I didn't care as one of the officers pulled me to the side with his clipboard in hand while Sergio was yelling that Brett was trying to kidnap me. I stared coldly at Brett as they dragged him off with handcuffs on his wrists. It gave me the chills that he continued to look at me even though they were taking him away. When he was finally tucked away in the car, I started to shake with relief.

"Now tell us what happened, ma'am," said the officer.

"He tried to kidnap me," I started.

AFTER DEALING WITH THE POLICE, Sergio carried me home in his arms after I insisted that I didn't require hospitalization. My mom hurriedly wrapped me in a quilt blanket when Sergio set me down on the couch. Two of my fathers, Caleb and Dravin, were home by now as Sergio recounted the story of what happened. Ian and Evan sat on either side of me, rubbing my back or petting my hair.

I felt comfortable with them after our many dates together. But I was still shaken after what happened.

"It's the end of him," said Ian. "I wish we killed him."

"I wish you did, too," I said, suddenly regretting stopping him. It would have all been in self-defense anyway, but I didn't want to risk it.

"Shoulda chopped off his pecker before he went to jail," growled Evan while my parents and Sergio talked quietly. I smiled despite my trembling limbs. "Well, this is the end of him, and you have nothing to worry about now."

"Thank god," I said, leaning against Evan while watching my mom pour tea for everyone in the room. "But now I'll be worried every night if he'll break out or something. You have no idea how weirdly obsessed he is."

"He won't," said Ian re-assuredly, rubbing my thigh.

"Are you okay?" asked Caleb, touching the scar on the right side of my face in concern. "I'm so sorry I wasn't there to save you. Once again. I blame myself for everything that happened to you."

"It's not your fault," I said. "I'm a grown omega, and I choose to go where I go. You can't protect me every single time, Dad."

Tears streamed down his face, and I was shocked to see that. I had never seen my dad cry like that. I slowly stood up and hugged him. He wrapped his arm around me and kissed my forehead.

"You will always be my baby," he said. "At least this pack of alphas can protect you, and you have my blessings if you wish to live with them."

"Thank you, Dad," I said, smiling. If I wanted to live with Sergio and his pack a long time ago, I would've done it. But I wanted to take things a little slower. "Don't blame yourself for anything that happens to me."

Thirty-Two

OLIVIA

Two Months Later

"More please," I said. I was lying across Sergio's lap as we watched a movie in his house. Ian handed me the bowl of candy, and I grabbed the sour gummies. I had craved it really badly throughout my pregnancy.

Evan and Sergio ate from the bowl of popcorn while I chewed on the deliciousness of the sour candy while watching the screen. I had finally agreed to watch their favorite Alpha Wars movie, even though I was bored half to death. But any time spent with the pack was wonderful to me. I enjoyed hanging out with them regardless of whether it was for a quick knotting, shopping, or dates.

"Looks like it's time," said Sergio, pausing the movie. "We need to get you back home before Caleb starts to worry."

"It's fine," I huffed. "He said it was fine for me to even live here."

"I don't want to lose his trust," said Sergio with finality in his tone.

"You just want to get rid of me," I whined, but he leaned down, kissing me hard on the lips.

"That's the last thing I want to do," he said, rubbing my tiny pregnant belly. "But I don't want to force you to stay or get the ire of your family on me."

"Aren't we going to knot one last time before you take me home?" I said, looking at the clock. It was only six p.m.

"Not tonight," said Sergio shortly, and I looked at him in surprise. He was never like this. And it felt like he was in a hurry to get rid of me.

"Oh, okay, that's fine," I said.

If he was going to act like this, then whatever. I would just ignore him. We had gotten into little disagreements here and there over the two months, but never like this. He was straight out refusing me, and I didn't like it.

Because it felt like a rejection to my omega soul.

I was unprepared for what would happen once we arrived at my parents' house.

"We're coming inside with you," said Sergio.

"But you never come inside," I said, confused.

"We do sometimes," said Ian, sounding hurt.

"Okay, that's fine if you want to talk to my fathers," I said nonchalantly as I stepped out of the car. As I walked towards the house, my mom greeted me at the door with a big smile.

"Hey, Libby," she said. "Sergio! Ian and Evan, come in."

"Hello, ma'am," greeted Sergio, giving her a hug. My mother hugged Evan and Ian next, giving Ian a peck on the cheek. My mother had a fondness for Ian and his boyish looks. If she had a son, I'm sure she'd want someone like him.

My fathers were home from their workday, roaming around the big house. They ran the Omega dating agency, interviewing singles on who they looked for in a partner. I knew they met my mom from that, and my mom's eyes never failed to twinkle when she told me the story each time. The house looked extra clean today, with candles lit and the fireplace on. The fire roared in the background as everyone came together, talking in the living room.

But my mom took me by the arm, "I need to talk to you."

"Okay," I said, following her to my room.

"Your fathers want to take you and your alphas out for dinner tonight," she said, and I groaned.

"Is that really necessary?" I said.

"Why? Are you upset with your alphas?"

"No," I said quickly, even though that was the true reason. "No wonder the house is suspiciously extra clean today and smelling nice."

"Are you saying it was stinky before?" she asked, looking affronted.

"No, Mom," I said, and she laughed.

"Anyways, I just wanted to let you know so you can put on something decent to wear," she said, looking at my casual attire of leggings and a shirt.

"Fine, I'll get dressed," I said, feeling tired after watching a movie with the pack. "I'm so tired, though."

"I know, darling. It comes with pregnancy," she said, her eyes glowing as she gazed at my stomach. "I absolutely can't wait to be a grandma."

"I know," I said, grinning.

"Wear the pink dress," she said hurriedly on her way out.

I sighed as I walked to my closest. Dinner with my fathers and my alphas sounded nice, but I didn't like how Sergio was trying to get rid of me so early. It wasn't even eight p.m., for goodness sake. Picking out the dress I wanted to wear, I draped it over my bed so I could straighten my hair.

While I straightened my hair, I heard the low rumble of

voices and laughter coming from downstairs. A feeling of tranquility settled over me at the sound. I liked it when my alphas bonded with my parents. Over the days, my dads had become more trusting of the alphas, especially after the incident with Brett.

When I put on the dress, I was glad it didn't fit too awkwardly over my small belly. The blush-colored dress clung to my body, and my hair was fanned down my shoulders. I had light pink lip gloss and eyeliner for a clean look.

It was simple but formal enough for a big family dinner.

I WENT DOWNSTAIRS to find my mom sitting in the living room, watching a cooking show on her own.

"Where's everyone?" I asked, and she sent off a quick text before turning to me. "Mom, what's going on? Are they in the car?"

"Yes, they're waiting outside," she said, walking to the back door towards our backyard.

"Did they park in the back?" I asked. I was so confused as I walked in my heels, following my mother outside. I gasped when I saw what was waiting outside. Each step towards the pavilion was adorned with candlelit lanterns, casting a warm and inviting glow along the way. "What the heck?"

"I'm glad you like it," giggled my mother as she led the way. As I approached, it looked like a fairy tale. The wooden beams were entwined with strings of twinkling fairy lights, casting a magical shimmer across the backyard.

My alphas, dressed in suits, stood around the central table, which was adorned with an exquisite display—a crystal vase overflowing with fresh blooms, their petals kissed by the glowing sunset in the sky. My fathers were throwing a white fabric over a canopy in the middle of work when we arrived.

"Ah, she's here early," said my dad, Bruce, and they struggled to finish up the project. When they were finished, the white fabric cascaded with grace.

Evan pulled a chair out for me as I approached, and I smiled, feeling like a queen.

"What an amazing surprise," I said, looking around at my family and the alphas who were grinning at me. "I never expected this."

"Anything for you, daughter," said Caleb gruffly. Then he winked at Sergio. "Enjoy your romantic dinner."

"Thank you, sir," said Sergio, his voice laced with nervousness, and I started to wonder why. Looking at the table, I saw four plates of food prepared for us. Shrimp and steak covered the plate, along with vegetables on the side. My mom had gone all out, cooking a spectacular meal for us.

"Wow, Mom, thank you," I said, smiling as I sat down. "Aren't you guys going to eat?"

"We will go inside," she said, grabbing both of her husbands' hands. "We'll see you in a little bit."

After they left, my alphas were in high spirits as we ate. I even forgot my little argument with Sergio during dinner.

"Did you guys organize this with my dads?" I asked curiously. "How did this happen?"

"I thought you'd feel more comfortable here than at some fancy restaurant for what I'm about to ask," said Sergio.

"Ask what?" I said. Then I dropped my fork in surprise when I saw all three alphas get up from their chairs and kneel on one knee before me with Sergio in the middle. My heart beat faster when Sergio pulled out a little red box from the inside of his blazer.

"With your family's blessings, I am here before you now," he started to the sound of low music playing on the radio. "My pack stands united, not only by the bond of brotherhood but also by the love and devotion we hold for you. I don't want to spend another day without you, Olivia Moonworth."

Tears streamed down my face as I watched him open the box containing a ring for me. An actual engagement ring. They didn't think I was too damaged to be with them, and my heart pounded furiously in my chest.

Evan and Ian were gazing at me with love in their eyes.

"Will you do me the honor of marrying myself and my pack?" continued Sergio. I was already nodding and crying as he slipped the ring onto my trembling finger.

"Yes," I said. "Yes to all of you."

I got up from the chair, hugging Sergio and kissing him on the lips to the cheers of my family in the background. I turned to kiss Ian and Evan next, who were equally as excited to marry me as I was to them. The ring was beautiful, with white and rose gold intertwined in an elegant braid, and in the center was a diamond surrounded by three gemstones of different vibrant colors.

The sapphire, ruby, and amethyst representing each alpha formed a colorful halo.

"Our omega fiance," said Ian.

"Will you move in with us then?" asked Evan, and my heart beat even faster at that question. It was a major commitment. But it was a commitment I was willing to take part in.

"Yes," I said, laughing as they all looked at me with shock in their eyes. "I love you all."

"We love you too, baby," said Ian, lifting me in his arms, and I squealed.

"Smile for the camera!" my mom said.

I looked up, seeing my mother ready with her camera, and I smiled as she took several pictures of me with my alphas. It was a peaceful, beautiful moment as I took pictures with my alphas and my dads cracking jokes with their future sons-in-law.

I will never forget tonight.

"Let's get your things packed," my mother said after we were done taking pictures. While the men laughed and talked outside, I joined my mom back into my bedroom. She magically pulled suitcases out of nowhere.

"You knew this was going to happen," I accused laughingly.

"I did," she said, unzipping the suitcases. "As long as you're happy about it, then I'm happy for you."

I lifted my clothes from the closet, dropping them into the suitcase. "Trust me, I'm happy. The alphas make me happy."

"I knew it," she said, carefully packing my accessories. "Your face glows when you're around them. Even before everything that happened to you, you seem happiest when you're with them."

Thirty-Three

OLIVIA

As we drove away from my childhood home, a sadness settled over me. I was going to miss home, but it had gotten to the point where I had to make a decision. And I didn't regret it. I had spent enough time with Sergio to know that I trusted him with my life.

My suitcases jumbled around in the trunk as we drove away.

"I can tell that you already miss being at home," said Ian, observing me in the darkness of the backseat.

"Not really," I said. "It's gotten too suffocating being at home with my parents since I'm their only child. It's about time I move out."

"It's okay to feel a little sad," said Ian.

"Okay, fine, I do," I said, and he tightened his hand around mine. I was going to miss my mother's cooking, painting with her, and writing in my room. The little life that I had known forever was gone now. Ian wrapped his arm around me while Evan gripped my right thigh.

It felt warm and comfortable being surrounded by them. As I played with the ring on my finger, my heart swelled when

I reminded myself that they were my fiances now. I was going to be a wife soon, and that feeling just felt right to me.

"Ah, we're to be married soon. I hope you're excited about wedding planning," said Sergio from the driver's seat.

"I am," I said. "We can start with the date first. Should we have our wedding before the baby or after?"

"I vote for after the baby is born," said Evan.

"Before the baby is born, so we can at least get freaky on our wedding night," winked Ian.

"What do you mean?" I asked, blushing.

"Oh, come on now, we all know how horny you get while pregnant."

"We'll have to figure out the details then, I guess," I sighed, already feeling overwhelmed. "We can just focus on the romantic night we'll have tonight."

"What idea do you have for tonight?" asked Sergio.

"Now that we're spending our first full night together, I want to do something special."

"Like spend the night in a five-star hotel?" asked Sergio, parking in front of the most well-known hotel on Howl's Edge. I gasped, seeing the bright lights twinkling from the glass of the building.

"I can't believe you did all this!" I said, awestruck. *Was this what having a pack felt like?* This night had taken a turn that I never thought would happen.

"It took months of planning for the proposal until your parents suggested doing it at their house," explained Sergio as we all stepped out of the car. He took my hand as Evan and Ian grabbed our suitcases. "I agreed because I knew you'd be more comfortable there than in front of a bunch of strangers out in public."

I swallowed a ball of emotion in my throat.

"Thank you," I whispered, and he squeezed my hand while he checked in at the front desk. The interior of the

Howl's Hotel was just as stunning as the outside. I had never stepped foot in here, and I was impressed. As we walked to our room, I could feel the throbbing between my legs grow worse with anticipation. I was horny already but also nervous.

"Baby, if you don't stop perfuming all over the place -I may have to rut you before we even get to the room," Sergio whispered in my ear, and I clenched my thighs together at his words. Every rustle of their suits against my arms sent tingles directly to my belly and down to my pussy. Every handhold and every kiss to my neck was electrifying. I was already a messy pool of slick between my thighs by the time we reached our room.

When we entered the room, I was surprised to see plates of sushi and fruit in the room. There was a small bowl filled with liquid chocolate and whipped cream on the side. Evan dipped a strawberry into the chocolate and brought it to my waiting mouth.

It was delicious and sweet, the juice bursting into my taste buds.

"Mhm," I said, standing next to the snack bowl with him as he fed me another bite. I hung onto his arm, batting my eyelashes as he fed me bite after bite of the strawberry.

"If you keep looking cute like that, I'm going to feed you forever," he growled, kissing me on the lips, even with chocolate all over my lipstick. Our kiss deepened as he led me towards the bed, laying me down on my back.

"She's all of ours tonight," said Sergio. "Sharing is caring, Evan."

"Fine," said Evan, reluctantly pulling off me. I saw Ian carrying the plates of sushi towards the bed with a naughty glimmer in his eyes. "What are you doing with that Ian?"

"I want to eat it off our omega's body," he said breathlessly, and I looked around to see that all of their cocks were hard, pants tented all around me.

"What?!" I asked, shocked. But the idea of it was slowly making me even more horny.

"Let's get that dress off you, shall we?" said Sergio, appearing in a flash beside me. I didn't realize how aroused they all were, so I turned onto my side like a good omega so he could unzip my dress. Innately, I wanted to please my alphas in bed. Outside of the bedroom, I was bossy, but inside the bedroom, it turned me on more to be submissive with alphas who cared about my well-being. "Let your alphas take care of you."

He deftly pulled my dress over my shoulders as Ian pulled it down my legs and off my feet. Evan unclasped my bra while Sergio ripped my underwear off. And just like that, I was laying on my back fully naked with my breasts out and my pussy on display for them. They used chopsticks to place the sushi onto my skin. The chilliness of it on my skin made my privates throb and clench uncontrollably.

Slowly, the men ate from the sushi that were laid on my breast, belly, thighs, and pussy. Sergio dipped the sushi between my legs, swirling it around my pussy, and I nearly clamped my legs in surprise. With his gaze on me, he ate the piece of sushi with relish. Then he proceeded to lick my pussy, and I almost convulsed with an already-impending orgasm.

"You taste better than the fucking sushi," he growled against my pussy while Evan and Ian sucked on my breasts.

He spread my thighs wider, and I felt my pussy folds open up before him. He liked to examine and lick my pussy if he wasn't playing with my ass.

And I enjoyed every second of it.

"I want to knot her pussy," said Ian, calling dibs.

"Fuck off," growled Sergio, who ate me out as I moaned and writhed on the bed. His tongue was powerful and meaty as he sucked my clit like it was a straw. "I need a taste of this pussy first."

Ian ignored him, kissing a trail down my breasts to my belly.

He was sucking every inch of my skin while Evan played with my hard nipples and squeezed my breasts together. In combination with Sergio licking my pussy, every nerve in my body came alive. I screamed as I climaxed around Sergio's lips on my clit. It was all too consuming, and at that moment, he plunged himself into my pussy. His huge body was above me as I turned to putty underneath him.

Thrust after thrust into my pussy.

His demanding cock stretched me wide as I moaned with pleasure. He thrust faster into me while Ian rubbed my clit with his little finger.

Each thrust of my pack leader's cock sent me higher until I couldn't take it anymore.

Clenching my pussy tight around him, I felt his cock stiffen and shoot inside of me. Then the wonderful knotting began as his cock swelled to an impossible proportion inside of me at the base. I tried to wriggle my pussy away, but his knot held me in place, pumping semen inside of me.

"Feels so fucking good," said Sergio, the wild look in his eyes dwindling to warm love as he pulled me onto my side to face him while we stayed knotted together.

"My favorite part is waiting for the knotting to go down," I said. "Because you're all mine."

Sergio laughed, "Are you saying I don't give you enough attention, omega?"

I raised my eyebrow, and he kissed me on the mouth to prevent me from saying anything. But while he was kissing me, I felt Ian and Evan's lips all over my ass, kissing my cheeks one at a time. Then I yelped when I felt a pair of hands separate my ass cheeks apart.

"I'm going to knot your tiny asshole while you're knotted to Serg," announced Evan impatiently.

"I'm not exactly used to that yet," I cried out, but he squeezed my ass cheeks in his desperation to have me.

Then he released my ass.

"Only if you want it," said Evan.

"Of course I want it," I said, breathing hard with arousal as I gripped Sergio's shoulder. "Just be gentle."

~

Evan

MY BREATHS GREW harsh and rapid as I spread her ass cheeks apart.

Her little hole clenched tightly the more I spread her ass cheeks apart. She looked so cute, knotted to our pack leader, and I couldn't help but do this now while she was knotted to him.

And I think Serg would appreciate the friction of her pussy grinding over him while I would thrust into her anus. Ian muttered something about clearing up the food, disappearing from the bed while I swirled my finger around her sphincter.

"Evan, you are freaky," she said, her voice muffled from her kiss with Sergio.

I blew air against her anus, causing her to clench her butt cheeks. But I held them apart, kissing each cheek slowly and sensually until I saw her hole start to relax.

Bringing my finger to her ass again, I rubbed her anus in circles, watching her release and clench. Then I felt the first drops of slick appear around her anus. That made me excited, and I quickly unzipped my pants, letting my cock free.

"Your ass is so adorable," I praised as I turned my attention back to it, rubbing her anus in circles.

"Thank you," she said shyly, and without seeing her face, I

knew she was red as a tomato. It turned me on that she was so shy with her ass. Omegas were capable of serving alphas with their ass just as their pussy without pain. But I would stop penetrating instantly if she felt any pain with my dick inside her tight hole.

"I'm going to enter your ass," I warned her as I placed the tip of my cock into her bottom. It was a mouth-watering delight to push into her tight warmth. Every push inside of her brought delight to my hard-as-fuck dick. As I lay on my side, I slowly stretched her as she held her breath.

Now fully inside, I groaned with pleasure and kissed the back of her shoulder.

"You're so huge," she moaned, throwing her head back, and I nibbled her ear as I began to thrust into her tightness. Each thrust inside her glorious little ass was heaven to my cock. Her hips pushed forward with each thrust of mine, and I could hear Sergio groan with his own pleasure at her pussy, squeezing his cock.

"So so nice," I growled, thrusting faster as she bounced between us alphas on the bed.

"Ah, love it when your tits hit me like that," groaned Sergio.

Her butt clenched around my cock, and I roared as I came inside her ass. My cock rapidly began swelling at the base, stopping her from moving away from me. Knotting inside her was the greatest pleasure an alpha could have.

"You're my omega," I growled into her ear, kissing her neck. "My omega forever."

"Yes," she said, breathing hard after I fucked her in the ass. "I'm yours. Yours to do as you wish. But only in bed."

I grinned at her bluntness. I was going to shower this omega with all the gifts in the world. Anything she wanted, I would give to her, no matter the price. She was my omega forever.

"I will cherish you until the day I die," I said, kissing her deeply on the neck until she moaned and closed her eyes, leaning into me as I hugged her.

~

Olivia

THE NEXT MORNING, Ian had a surprise for me once we were back home at the pack house. While I was in the middle of slipping on green silk robes, Ian appeared at the doorway, watching me apply eyeliner.

"Are you getting dressed up for me?" he asked, coming towards me and kissing my neck.

"Just a tiny bit," I said, warmth creeping up my face. Ian's blond hair mingled with my hair as he pressed his cheek to mine, looking into the mirror with me.

"You look beautiful just the way you are," he said. "Your dark eyelashes, honey-brown eyes, and wet curly hair are enough to set any alpha ablaze. You are a beauty all on your own."

"Why thank you, Mister Ian," I breathed. I set down the eyeliner and turned to kiss him on the lips. "Should we celebrate our engagement now? I've already *celebrated* with Evan and Sergio. So I'm in need of your knot."

"Before we do that," he said huskily. "I've arranged a small surprise for you, my love. And I got rid of Sergio and Evan to have you to myself."

"Oh, did you?" I asked, pleasantly surprised.

"I sure did," he said. "Take my hand."

I tightened the rope around my bathrobe and took his hand as we walked out of the room. We went down the stairs, and he led me towards a room that I hadn't been in before. I just assumed it was one of the guy's bedrooms or office space.

"Close your eyes," he said, and I did. For some reason, I was nervous about what to expect. I heard the door opening and then, "Open your eyes, baby."

I gasped.

The blue bookshelves stole my breath away. They were filled with books from top to bottom. The best part about the room was the cute hammock and the chair with a desk. And in the back of the room roared a blazing fireplace.

"Oh my god," I said, stunned.

"This is for you," said Ian. "I've been quietly working on this at nights after you went back to your family's home. Do you like it?"

"Of course I do!"

I beelined into the room, running my fingers over the spines of the books. Deliciously thick books that I would love to sink my teeth into at night. My heart pounded with excitement at the thought of writing my stories in here, too, with the fireplace roaring behind me on cold days.

I turned to Ian and stood up on my tippy toes to kiss him. He kissed me back, cupping and squeezing my ass in his hands as he held me to him. A wave of love and warmth filled me while I kissed him.

"Well shit," said Ian when I finally released him. "Typically, I'm not interested in books or anything, but I'm glad you're over the moon about it."

"I am," I said, grinning, pulling him towards the fireplace. I untied my robes and allowed it to slowly drift to the floor. His eyes widened as he gazed at my naked body. Nervousness went through me as I lowered myself to the ground onto my back and spread my legs wide. But the nervousness soon turned into arousal as he gazed at my open pussy. I slowly rubbed my pussy in front of him, which was already shining with slick.

"Fuck," he said huskily, kneeling between my legs and

unbuckling his belt. I heard the belt and his pants drop to the ground as he eagerly lowered his head between my legs.

My breathing quickened when I felt his tongue slide across my pussy.

"Oh, moons," I moaned as he licked me in slow, lazy circles over my clit.

"Mhm, you taste so good," he said. "If I knew giving you a library would have this effect on you, I would've done it every day."

"I'm yours," I reminded him.

"That's right," he growled, his eyes rolling back as he kissed my clit. The force of his lips made me tremble. "And I'm yours, babe."

"So knot me then," I said.

"You don't need to ask me twice."

He suddenly thrust inside me, stretching my pussy instantly. It felt so good as he thrust in and out in a glorious rhythm before the fireplace. Our breaths mingled and collided just like our bodies.

Joining as one.

"Ian," I cried out when my pussy throbbed uncontrollably, spasming around his cock. Slick drenched my thighs as fireworks went through me. He continued to plunge into my pussy. Faster and harder until we both cried out in ecstasy.

"Damn," he growled as he released copious amounts of semen inside of me. Sharp, hot blasts of liquid went straight into me as his cock knotted us together before the fireplace. We lay there, breathing hard and sweaty before the fire, staring into each other's eyes. "I'll make a second library for you very soon."

I giggled and smacked him on his hairy chest.

"I swear it's not that," I protested.

"Oh, it is," he said. Then he wiggled his eyebrows. "What do you read in those books, I wonder?"

Thirty-Four

SERGIO

I was back at the OBC two days after my engagement with our omega, Olivia. I had to find my mother's grave, wherever Henry had buried her.

The buildings were deserted, and it looked like a ghost town when I arrived. The sand crunched under my thick boots as I walked around the perimeter. My hand was on my gun, just in case any of the old guards were hiding out here. I couldn't believe I spent years here, trapped and unable to leave after not finding my mother. Henry made sure that the alphas didn't just leave and expose the operation he was running here.

I hoped that motherfucker was dead. That would be the greatest news.

As I walked towards the prisoners' barracks, I looked around the back of the buildings and finally saw it.

There was a small plot of land with rocks embedded into the sand in a rectangular formation and a yellow crime tape around it all. Slowly, I took a look at each of them, and upon closer inspection, I could see names and initials marked on the largest stone.

Inspecting each grave, I saw various names of different

females and small infant graves, which bore heavily on my soul. All the crimes Henry committed right here for everyone to see. My breathing paused when I saw her name scratched faintly onto the biggest rock.

I'd found it. My mother's grave.

Tears sprung to my eyes as I dropped to my knees in front of the grave. I laid my palms against the dirt, and my tears soaked the sand under me. Just being here, I could feel all the pain and suffering she went through. Her baby son, me, was taken away from her in such a brutal way.

"I wish I had known you, Mother," I whispered. "You are everything to me even if I'd never met you. I was raised well by good parents who took care of me just as you wanted. But I came back for you, and now it's too late. I love you."

I closed my eyes tight, seeing her in my mind's eye, screaming for her baby.

Chills went through me to the bone, and I could almost hear her voice in the wind telling me she loved me back. I lost it right there, sobbing uncontrollably as I knelt over the dirt. Henry had destroyed the only family I ever had, and I couldn't care less who my father was - the alpha who raped my mother. I didn't want to face the fact that I was the child of a brute.

I felt a small hand rubbing my shoulder, and I knew it was my omega by her cherry scent. As she stood behind me, I gripped her hand in mine without turning. She sniffled, and I knew she was crying as well.

"I'm so sorry," said Liv, kissing me on the cheek, and I could feel her wet tears on my face. "I wish she was here with us."

I nodded without saying a word as tears fell onto the dirt. The rest of my pack had shifted, in wolf form, as they stood around my mother's grave, grieving along with me in silence. Later, we would have to go for a run as wolves. I needed it, and so did my pack.

Olivia

THE RIDE HOME WAS SOMBER.

I felt for Sergio, and I wished he had gotten to know his mother. The camp disappeared behind us as we drove in the night. We had been at the camp for most of the day, and I watched the alphas from afar as they ran off the emotion they were feeling. Thankfully, I had brought sandwiches to stave off my nausea, but I was feeling hungry again.

Living full-time with the alphas was an easier adjustment than I thought. They gave me space whenever I needed it, and pregnancy had made me more horny than usual, so it was nice to have an alpha ready to rut me on command. They were more than excited the minute I said I needed a knot, so it had been fun.

Wedding planning had gone by the wayside since I was sick in the mornings, and I couldn't gather the energy to even think of planning a wedding right now.

"We're home," said Evan after the long ride back from the OBC.

"Good, because I'm hungry," I sighed. Ian opened my door and held my hand as we walked to the house. I was familiar now with the pink and red rosebushes in front of the home, and I couldn't wait to add my own plants to the collection.

In the middle of cooking dinner, I started to feel sick at the smell of the onions frying in the pan. Ian was busily chopping up cubes of meat as I hunched over the trash.

"Are you okay, Liv?" said Sergio, rushing into the kitchen.

"Just feel a little sick, that's all," I heaved as I tried to hold the contents back in my stomach.

"Go lay down on the couch," he ordered, and I didn't

need to be told twice. "Evan! Come here and finish cooking. I need to take care of Liv."

I slowly made my way to the couch, holding my belly.

The fresh air flowing through the windows was a nice reprieve as I lay on the couch. I opened all the windows in the house every time I cooked, but it never seemed to clear out the food smell.

I closed my eyes, breathing in the fresh air.

"Cold lemonade for you, my love," said Sergio, pressing a cold glass to my lips. I opened my eyes, taking a sip of the cold strawberry drink. It was refreshing, and the sickness began to subside. "I don't want you cooking in the kitchen anymore if you feel sick."

"You got it, pack leader," I said, and he grinned, kneeling in front of the couch as he made me take another sip. Grabbing the remote, I turned the TV on to watch the news with him.

"Breaking news," said the female reporter on the screen. *"It has been found that several omegas had been taken by the mastermind Henry while escaping the raid. It is unclear how many omegas he had kidnapped as they haven't been accounted for. Twenty alphas associated with the crimes are still at large. Their mode of escape, speedboats, had been reportedly seen in the water by sight-seers."*

"So fucking horrible," said Sergio, while softly touching my belly.

"What do you think he plans to do with them?" I asked, contemplating the horrors that the omegas might be forced to endure.

"Nothing good," he said. "I don't want you to stress about that. God knows how much stress you've already been through."

"I just hope they're okay."

"I know, baby," said Sergio, kissing me on the lips. "But all this stress can't be good for the baby. How about let's change the channel to something else and play a game of chess while our pack cooks us dinner?"

I smiled, "a huge alpha playing chess?"

"Just like I played puzzles with you," he growled. "I enjoy it. And I know you love it even more."

THE NEXT DAY, I never imagined who was going to walk into my home as I quietly wrote my story in my notebook.

"Hey Olivia," said a soft female voice, and I shut my notebook closed, looking up to see Lacy standing there in a flowing pink dress, her belly about ready to pop. She was holding candles and oils in her hands, which she slowly set down on the coffee table. "I know you probably still hate me, but your alphas had told mine that you were experiencing morning sickness."

"Isn't that normal?" I said, not sure what to do with my cousin. We weren't exactly talking like buddies, like how we used to. Text messages had gone silent, and there were no more calls between us.

"It is, but there are ways to make yourself feel a little better," she said, handing me a roll-on made with peppermint and lavender oil. "Just roll this over your stomach and your chest in the morning and at night. I could swear by it."

"Oh, cool, thanks I guess," I said, staring at the bottle in my hand. "I'll try it later, I suppose. Listen about the hiking trip..."

"No, I'm sorry," said Lacy, cutting me off quickly before I could speak. "I wish I waited until you were rescued to have my wedding. And I should have tried more to save you."

"I know you tried," I said. "I'm sorry too for a lot of stuff I said out of anger. You deserve to be happy, too."

I thought about all the omegas who were still not found and the helplessness I felt watching the news last night. It was bigger than I could have ever thought of.

"So all forgiven?" she asked hopefully.

"Only if you sing at my wedding," I said, smiling.

"You got it," said Lacy, grinning at me. It was a moment of shared forgiveness, which was the best feeling to have right now. She immediately sat next to me and hugged me from the side. I leaned into her, sensing her ginger scent.

"Your perfume makes me feel less sick," I said, and she laughed.

"Your ring!" she exclaimed, pulling my hand.

"Yes, I'm engaged now," I said, smiling.

"Oh my god, congratulations," she said, with tears in her eyes.

Throughout the rest of the day, she spent time in my house as we caught up on everything that happened to us. She cried with me when I told her about what I had gone through at the camp. And I laughed with her at her outrageous wedding led by a clown singer that she was obsessed with. Even her husband, Adrian, was hanging out with my alphas outside.

It was a peaceful day, and when she left, I went to my room to try the oil. I was lying on my back, pulling my dress up over my thighs and exposing my stomach.

"Ooh, what's going on here?" asked Evan in a naughty voice.

"I need to put the oil on," I explained breathlessly, trying to open the cap.

"Allow me to put it on for you," he said, unscrewing the cap in two seconds and slowly rubbing it over all over my skin. "You're so incredibly beautiful."

I started to feel aroused as he rubbed the oil sensually over my belly and my thighs next. The sharp smell cleared my brain and my senses.

"I think it's working already," I said in wonderment as he put away the oil. He lay next to me and grasped my face with one hand, kissing me on the lips.

"I'm so glad because I miss sexy time," he said, and my pussy throbbed as he grasped my breast through my bra.

"You're turning me on," I accused.

"Is that so?" he asked with an arched eyebrow.

Epilogue

OLIVIA

Three Years Later

As I stared at my bridesmaids ahead of me, I was growing more nervous by the second. I could hear Lacy's melodic voice singing a slow wedding tune outside where the guests sat. We stood inside the cool building, waiting for the door to open, leading outside for my beach-themed wedding. I was barefoot, and I couldn't wait for my feet to get warm in the sand waiting outside.

"You're nervous," said my dad, Caleb, holding my left arm while my other dad, Bruce, held my right arm.

"I know it's weird since I already live with them and all," I said, playing down my emotions like I always did. "I shouldn't be nervous."

"It's okay to feel nervous," said Bruce. "I felt the same with your mother. You will feel like this when you're about to marry the true love of your life. And then a peace will come over you."

"Thanks, Dad," I said, and he squeezed my arm when the double doors finally opened ever so slowly.

Natural sunlight streamed into the grand hallway, and the bridesmaids made their way outside, looking stunning in their soft purple dresses. Reyna and Alana's two younger sisters, Roxanne and Sarah, were my bridesmaids. I wanted to include Reyna since she had been such an amazing support during all my group therapy sessions.

I looked behind me and smiled at my son, Cassius, who was holding the rings on a small cushion. I smiled. He was focused intently on the cushion so it didn't drop, but my mother was right next to him to make sure it all went smoothly. I had planned this wedding for so long, and now I was scared of messing anything up.

We started to walk, and my heart pounded in my chest as we walked down the aisle lined with lilies. Around two hundred guests sat in wooden chairs adorned with pastel ribbons, matching the vibrant floral arrangements.

A rustic wooden arch embellished with blooms and foliage stood over the three alphas who were ready to marry me. My A-line dress flowed in a whisper against the sand as I walked to them, and upon looking up, my eyes caught all three of my alphas. They stood in neatly pressed suits, with different colored ties matching my ring.

Butterflies swirled in my belly as we walked up to the arch, and now I was finally standing in front of the three of them. I gave them a small nervous smile, and Sergio had tears forming in his eyes when my fathers released me.

"Take care of our daughter," said Caleb.

"Always," nodded Sergio.

My fathers made their way back to their seats, and the officiant cleared his throat while holding the microphone. I briefly glanced at all our guests. All my mother's friends were here, along with their alphas and children, which made for a huge gathering. I accidentally caught the eye of Alana and Lio, sitting next to their three children, and she gave me a wide smile, her eyes twinkling. Lacy was on the stage with her two beta bandmates, playing a slow song as the officiant read from a piece of paper. Her baby girl, Francine, was sitting on Vanessa's lap, her curly hair just as red as her mother's.

It was time for the alphas to say their vows and my heart was beating erratically when Sergio stepped forward first, clasping my hands in his.

"You are my first love and the coolness of my heart," said Sergio. "As pack leader, I vow to cherish and honor you. I pledge to protect you and support you with all that I am."

He released my hands, and tears shimmered in my eyes as our gazes lingered on one another. Then Ian stepped forward, grasping my hands next.

"Olivia Moonworth," he started, and I smiled at the seriousness of his tone. He had never been so serious before with me, and I found it touching. "My love, my omega. You are the essence of beauty and courage. You are much stronger than I could ever be in spirit, but I promise to make you stronger with my protection. If any other alpha outside of our pack comes near you, I'll slice his head off. Not anyone in this crowd, of course..."

The guests all laughed at that one, and I giggled at his brazenness. He kissed the back of my hands before releasing me. I was trying not to cry, but tears poured down my cheeks despite my efforts not to ruin my makeup.

It was Evan's turn now as he clasped my hands in his, "My Olivia. You bring light into my life like no other. I would love to dance all the dances with you, and I pledge to be your steadfast companion and to be your alpha till death do us part."

Then the officiant turned to me, "Do you, in the presence of these alphas, take them to be your partners in life? To love, honor, and cherish, for as long as you all shall live?"

I took a deep breath, gazing at all three men who loved me with all their hearts. I could feel their love radiating in the air around me, their alpha scents thick with emotion as they gazed at me.

"I do," I said, smiling and crying.

I WAS surprised out of my mind when I saw what the alphas planned for our honeymoon.

"A plane?!" I shouted amongst the whirring of the blades.

The white plane was polished and looked majestic as the boarding stairs extended gracefully. As my alphas escorted me to the plane, I looked back at my mom, holding my son in her arms, and he was crying. I had never been away from my son for more than a day.

"It's only three days," said Ian in my ear. "I know I'm hurting too about leaving him. But your mama will take care of him."

"She will," I said, comforting myself more. Ian squeezed my hand, and I took a deep breath as I walked up the stairs, waving at everyone one last time. Our reception party was beautiful, and it was amazing dancing with my alphas. We had a pile of gifts given to us by the guests, and my fathers had offered to bring it to our home while we were gone.

The entrance of the plane revealed a glimpse of the lavish interior adorned with plush seating, elegant fixtures, and soft ambient lighting. It was even fancier than the private plane we took to escape the omega breeding camp.

Upon entering, there was a circular sitting area that held comfortable chairs and even a small couch that was fastened to the floor securely. I sat in the middle of Ian and Sergio on the couch, admiring the light of the sunset shining through the windows.

"Do you like it?" asked Sergio.

"All I'm wondering is, how the heck did you do all this? Where are you taking me?" I asked, still in shock as I took in my surroundings. I was wearing a thinner white dress from our reception party, and the silk fabric was hot against my skin.

"The government owes us a small pittance, and I'm sure you'll be getting a fair share of your money soon," explained Sergio. "After the OBC incident."

"Oh," I said. "But I wouldn't waste it on private jets or vacations."

"This is our honeymoon, sweetie," said Ian, kissing my cheek. "We wanted it to be special because we love you."

I smiled against his lips when I turned to kiss him.

"I appreciate it, but I really don't need all this," I sighed. Evan held a chocolate bar to my mouth, and I gratefully took a bite.

"Our little omega is hungry, that's all," he said gruffly, and I rolled my eyes. "Don't ever take the bait, alphas."

"My feelings about your lavish spending *are* real," I protested, but he fed me another bite, and my eyes rolled back in delight. "So scrumptious."

Sergio laughed, kissing the chocolate from my lips, and Ian purred against my neck, calming me.

"This is our honeymoon, sweetheart," said Sergio. "Just relax and let us spoil you."

"Oh my god," I said, falling for their purring, petting and kissing. "Fine, I'll let go of it. Just because you fed me some chocolate doesn't mean it's all over."

"Yes, honey," said Evan, making me lick the melted chocolate off his fingertips, and his breathing grew thicker. His cock jutted from his pants as I sucked on his middle finger. Then he whispered harshly, "Keep doing that, and I'll knot inside your mouth in front of the flight attendant."

I gasped at his audacity, releasing his finger.

"I just want a little fun," I whined, acting innocent as I batted my lashes at him.

"Fuck, how long until we reach there?" growled Evan as Sergio held him back by the chest.

"Won't be for another hour at least," said Sergio. "Chill. Sit down and drink something cold."

"Don't act like you're not ready to knot her, too," said Evan, and I looked down at Sergio's private area. He was indeed hard. Then I looked over at Ian and realized he was just as horny, and my pussy throbbed.

My heart started beating faster. *Oh damn*, I was in for some wedding night knotting.

WHEN I STEPPED out of the helicopter, my jaw dropped. We were on a different island of sorts, and it didn't have anyone on it.

Ahead of us was a massive castle I had never seen before.

"Oh my god," I said, at a loss for words as the alphas stared proudly at the spot they had chosen.

The tropical palm trees were planted on each side of the castle, their leaves brushing against the walls. There was a spiral stone staircase on the outside of the castle, and it looked like historical magnificence. It had always been my dream to write in such an old, historic place like this. I could already feel the ghosts of the past whispering to me as we walked towards it.

"Do you like it?" asked Ian. "Wait until you see the inside."

"It's amazing," I breathed as Ian and Evan held my hands while Sergio led the way, giving out long explanations of the landmarks around us. Upon entering the castle, I was taken aback by the historical opulence and the grand purple curtains. "What is this place?"

"It was where the great General of the Greenstone Pack lived," explained Sergio with excitement. "He and his pack died serving for our kingdom. Now, his castle is used for alpha packs needing a vacation, sightseeing, or for celebrations. We're not far from Howl's Edge at all."

I stared in wonder at the beautiful living room.

A chandelier, adorned with a myriad of crystals, cast prisms of light that painted the marble floors with a dazzling display. The gentle glow from candelabras and sconces lining the walls added a warm, inviting atmosphere to the place.

The flight attendants had brought in our suitcases and left them at the door as we walked further in. The huge spiraling staircase set my heart aflutter as I gazed at the ancient art carved into the golden handrails.

"I love it so much," I said, carried away by the beauty of this house.

Sergio climbed up the steps after me as I traced the carving on the handrail. "We thought you might like it, considering that you like to write historical romance and all."

"I just want to live here forever," I sighed, and the three alphas chuckled. Sergio suddenly swooped me off my feet, carrying me in his arms the rest of the way to the grand bedroom.

I pressed a hand on his chest, trying to unbutton his shirt as he carried me. There was so much sexual tension between us earlier with the entire wedding and the ride here. My underwear was drenched by now, especially from Ian's purring into my neck earlier.

Upon entering the bedroom, Sergio gently set me down on the huge bed. All three alphas started ripping off their suits as I stared wide-eyed at them.

Belts, shirts, and pants lay scattered around the beautiful large room.

A huge dresser with a majestic mirror sat in the room across the bed. I admired the shiny gold headboard with intricate flower patterns carved into it. Directly above the bed was a stunning chandelier covered in crystals.

When I looked back down, I didn't realize three muscular alphas suddenly surrounded me. Sergio sat to my right and Ian to my left while Evan sat behind me. Evan pulled me onto his chest while Ian and Sergio gently caressed my arms.

"We are going to make love to you tonight," said Sergio. "To show you how much we love you."

"As your new husbands," said Ian. "Don't forget that."

"Tonight, we will mark and claim you as ours," whispered Evan as my stomach somersaulted with nervousness.

Marking an omega was an ancient tradition, meant to communicate to other alphas that I was a taken omega since we were rare. It would also mean that I would be bonded to these alphas for life, and if one of us were to walk away from the other, we would experience the pain and heartbreak much more than the average relationship. The pain would only stop if one of the partners were to die.

Our union tonight would be for life. And I was excited because of how much I trusted and loved them with all my heart.

"I can't wait," I breathed, laying my head back against Evan's chest as I ran my hands along Sergio's and Ian's chests. Their chests were defined with muscles, and it made it impossible to think clearly in the haze of their alpha scents mixed with the smell of cologne.

"You're perfuming," said Sergio, pressing his nose to my neck. "You smell like cherries."

I could feel Evan unzipping my white dress from behind and Ian carefully pulling down my lace sleeves. Soon, my dress was on the floor, joining all of their discarded clothes. I was only wearing a white bra now and thin white panties as they kissed me everywhere. Kisses from Evan rained down my shoulders, my neck, and my back. Ian and Sergio kissed thighs, belly, and arms.

But Evan expertly unclasped my bra from behind, and Ian tossed it to the floor.

"Her breasts are much bigger," said Sergio in appreciation while I blushed like crazy.

"Especially after childbirth," said Ian, weighing my breast in his hand while Sergio squeezed my other breast. Evan had a hold of my ass cheeks from behind, squeezing and releasing me.

Waves of desire streamed through my belly and down my legs in the form of slick.

"I smell your slick," growled Sergio, immediately separating my legs. "You might be in pre-heat very soon, my love."

My breaths came out faster and harsher as he placed his fingers under the waistband of my panties. As he fondled my pussy, I felt myself clenching as I laid back against Evan to give him access.

"I need to touch her pussy too," said Ian, and they suddenly ripped my panties open in the middle. My breasts heaved up and down in arousal as they both played with my pussy.

Evan reached around my waist and started rubbing my clitoris.

"Oh fucking moons," I moaned, seeing stars as my eyes rolled back with the intense pleasure they were giving me. I soon lost track of where each person's fingers were as I rode their fingers.

"Fuck, look at how much slick she's releasing," said Sergio, plunging his finger into me with a loud squelch. Another finger was spreading my labia open as Sergio thrust his finger in and out of me.

"Oh!" I shouted as I felt it coming. The waves of pleasure crashed over me, drowning me in delight as I squirmed, my pussy throbbing and clenching around their merciless fingers. "Stop, that's enough, please."

I was panting and clenching when Sergio popped his finger out of my vagina, licking his fingers. The rest of the alphas proceeded to do the same, and my face turned hot with embarrassment, listening to them slurping my slick off their fingers.

"Our wife tastes so good," groaned Evan. "I need to knot inside her already."

"Patience, wolf," admonished Sergio, climbing over my sweaty body. He kissed my breasts while his hardened dick rubbed against my thighs.

Evan held me onto him from behind as Sergio kissed me on the mouth. Our lips meshed and danced over each other. His tongue teased at my lips, plunging into my mouth while his cock slipped into my pussy. I cried out at the impact, and he kissed away my moans. His dick seemed to have gotten bigger as he pushed even further inside of me, stretching my pussy.

The fullness of him felt so good.

"Oh moons," I gasped out loud when he began to thrust into me, trapping my hands onto the bed with his own. While his cock speared into me over and over, Ian nibbled on my breasts, playing with both of them. Evan had spread my ass cheeks, teasing the entrance to my anus with his fingers. Sergio's eyes glowed orange in the dark, and his body gleamed with muscles from the candlelight flickering.

He grunted loudly with each thrust, his face intense as he took me.

"He's fucking her hard," said Ian out loud as he watched

me. My pulse quickened even more while he watched the pack leader make love to me. Suddenly, Sergio leaned forward, pressing his sharp canine teeth against my shoulder.

I braced myself as he punctured my skin, and I cried out.

The electricity of desire swirled through me, igniting my body as I moaned from my instant orgasm. He also climaxed after one last one hard thrust into my pussy. He roared, exploding hot bursts of semen inside of me.

Sergio hugged me as he licked the burn from my right shoulder.

"I'm sorry if that hurt," he said gruffly.

"It wasn't that bad," I said, breathing hard underneath him while his penis knotted to me. "At first, it stung, but after that, it was fine."

"Good," said Sergio, kissing me again on the mouth after licking my small wound. "You're my omega now, forever."

"Forever and ever," I finished, and he grinned.

"You're so cute," he said, kissing my neck gruffly. "I can't get enough of you. Especially now that you're my wife."

As I lay with Sergio during the knotting, I could sense the impatient need emanating from Ian and Evan. So as soon as Sergio's knot released me, Ian sat between my legs while Evan sat me on his lap again, and I could feel his hard cock stirring underneath me.

"We will take you at the same time," said Ian, and Evan growled in agreement. "I know it's not your ideal wedding night knotting."

"You know I love it," I said breathlessly at the thought of being sandwiched between two giant knots in bed. "I think I'm up for it."

"Perfect," said Evan, pushing his cock between my ass cheeks while Ian did the same to my pussy. They both thrust in at the same time, and I gasped out loud at the instant intrusion. The stretching of my pussy and ass at the same time felt amazing. The feeling of fullness dominating over me was incredible.

"God, your pussy is full of our leader's semen," groaned Ian. "So wet and juicy inside. So fucking tight."

"Her ass is amazing," groaned Evan, pushing further and further into my butt.

"You might be too big!" I yelped when he thrust his dick all the way into my ass. "You haven't stretched my ass in days."

"I know, baby. It's my fault," Evan said as I gasped breathlessly against Ian's mouth. Ian was slowly thrusting in and out of my pussy while Sergio watched us, propped up on his elbow and sporting another erection.

"This is incredibly hot," said Sergio, watching me bounce between them. His eyes were hooded and laced with dark lust. "I need to rut her from behind after you both are through with her."

My pussy clenched when he said that, and Ian smiled devilishly.

"You like when he talks dirty to you?" said Ian. "Because your pussy is telling me that you do."

My face burned with embarrassment.

"Kind of," I gasped when he pistoned into me, his hips jackhammering against mine. Evan and Ian moved in a rhythm on each side of me, skin against skin. Their warm muscles brushing against my hot skin felt so good. Their dicks inside me moved at the same time, thrusting and pulling at the same time.

Until it was time for them to mark me...

Ian placed his mouth on my left shoulder while Evan did the same to my neck. At the same time, their sharp teeth punctured my skin, causing the same electricity to flow to my belly but with double the force. I orgasmed, screaming out their names as I shattered around their angry cocks inside my pussy and ass. Ian roared through his orgasm while Evan grunted heavily behind me, spurting warmth into my anus. Before any of their liquid could spill out, their cocks knotted to me, preventing any of it from going to waste.

"So fucking amazing," breathed Ian. "She's ours, and it feels much different now after marking her."

"It does," agreed Evan.

"I feel it too," I said, more in tune with their emotions somehow. I felt much more at home and relaxed around them. "I feel like I'm home."

"I do, too," said Sergio, who was lying at my head while I was sandwiched between Ian and Evan. He kissed my forehead. "I will never feel at home unless you're there with us, omega. You are a part of us as we are of you. Our omega forever."

Tears gathered in my eyes, and Ian quickly kissed my tears away.

"Don't cry, sweetheart," said Ian while Evan kissed my shoulders. "This is the happiest moment of my life."

"Mine too," agreed Evan, giving me endless pecks along my collarbone.

"I'm not crying. They're happy tears," I said, smiling. Sergio kissed me on the lips while he hovered above me. As I lay snuggled with all three of them on my wedding night, I was glad for the first time that I ended up at the omega camp despite the situations I was put in. Because if I had never been there, I would never have found my one true pack who loved me like they did.

"I love you all," I said breathlessly, taken aback by their muscular bodies surrounding every inch of me.

"We love you too, Liv."

THE END

Thank you for reading! I hope you enjoyed this series. *Guess what?* The journey doesn't end here.

My next book follows the journey of Treasure's daughter years later, growing up in Henry's new society.

Born without a scent and deemed a beta at birth, will she survive being a servant of society for life? Things take a turn when she ends up working for a pack of alphas who just can't seem to keep their hands off of her.

Read the first book here in my brand-new series! Maid for The Alphas: Dawn of The Alphas (Book 1)

Also By Layla Sparks

Howl's Edge Island: Omega For The Pack (COMPLETED Reverse Harem Series)

Book 1 (*Tiana's story*): Stolen by The Pack

Book 2 (*Keera's story*): Auctioned to the Pack

Book 3 (*Lyra's story*): Princess For The Pack

Book 4 (*Vanessa's story*): Betrayed by The Pack

Book 5 (*Jade's story*): Matched to The Pack

Book 6 (*Alana's story*): Knotted by The Pack

Book 7 (*Lacy's story*): Craved by The Pack

Book 8 (*Olivia's story*): Freed by The Pack

Dawn of The Alphas: Omega For The Pack Series

Book 1: Maid for The Alphas *(Breanna's story)*

Book 2: <u>Promised to The Alphas</u> *(Ruby's story)*

Book 3: <u>Denied by The Alphas</u> *(Carmen's story)*

The Librarian and Her Alphas *(Standalone Reverse Harem)*

9 798230 107323